I0523830

The Dahlia

Jane's Story

Novella
The Hunterson Cavalier Heir

KRISTEN DOVNIK & LAUREN LUKA

DEDICATION

This is for the two little girls who used to constantly fight over everything who grew up to become best friends.

BOOKS BY KRISTEN DOVNIK

<u>The Chronicles of the Light Princess</u>
Conflictus
Contentment

Revelations

Symador (Charity Anthology)

<u>The Hunterson Cavalier Heir</u>
The Dahlia (Novella)

GRANDESSA
ENCHANTED COVE
MOSSIDARIA
THE MOSS
MILL

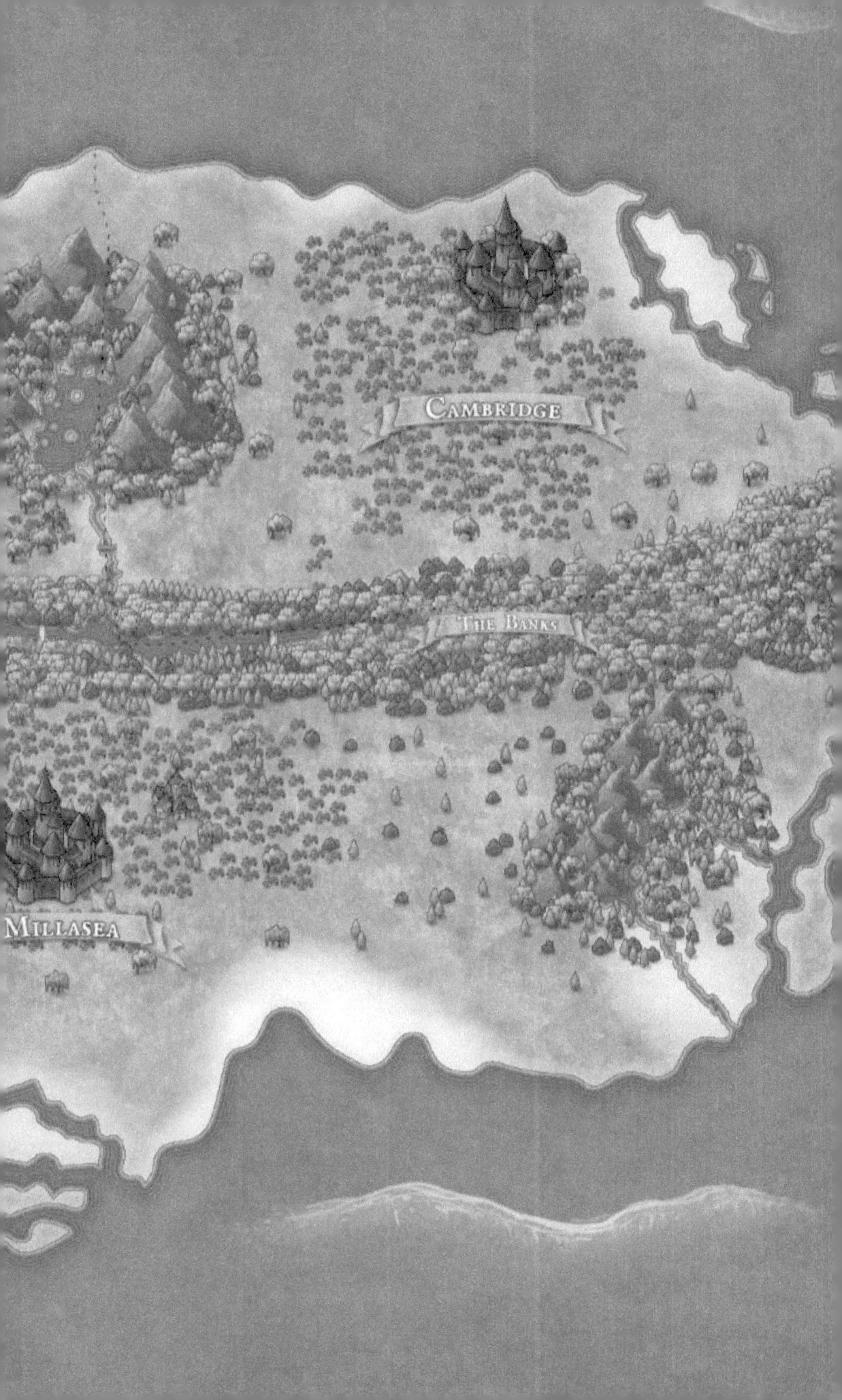

CAMBRIDGE
THE BANKS
MILLASEA

The sea breeze glides over my face as I stare over the horizon. Watching the waves crash into the shore usually calms my nerves, but not today. It is my twenty-first birthday and tomorrow night is my coming out party. It is at this party that I am required to choose and announce my future husband, the man that I will spend the rest of my life with. My father has composed a list of eligible bachelors that meet his approval and I must choose my future husband from this list. I already know the man that I want and to my relief, his name is on the list that my father presented to me. There is just one problem though, my heart and body craves him; but he has never really shown any interest in me, in that way.

From the moment William and I met, he has been on my mind. I'll never forget the day that he stumbled into the markets, knocking over a stack of chicken pens, ultimately releasing chaos into the market square. We raced through the stalls laughing, as we attempted to catch the runaway chickens. It was the most fun I have ever had and the memory brings a smile to my face. We have been the best of friends since and while my fondness for him has only grown over the years; a continual burn for someone to be close to you and a want to share your innermost thoughts with them, I don't know if he feels the same.

I rub my hands up and down my arms as the early afternoon breeze starts to chill. I know it's almost time to go but I will stand here and wait until the very last second, enjoying the peace the ocean brings me. Birds chirp high over my head as I continue to watch the waves, before they alter their course and dive into the water, retrieving their dinner. If only my life were that simple.

I am to be the Duchess of Mossidaria. Once I am wed, my mother's title will then fall to me and I will rule over the people surrounding our estate. My reign will not be on such a scale as Cambridge or Millasea but the responsibility of overseeing so many people is daunting.

Another cool breeze touches my skin, sending a shiver running down my spine. I despise the last vestiges of winter; it is always colder now, than it was in the middle of the season. I can't wait for spring. To be able to spend every waking moment down here lounging in the warm sun. To be able to go for a swim and not freeze my ass off.

"Jane dear, it's time to go," My mother calls from the ridge behind me. I let out a sigh. Why must we leave already? I know it's a bit of a distance back to our estate but I don't want to go. My stomach drops at the thought of entering the ballroom tomorrow night and having all those people stare at me. Everyone is anxiously waiting to see who I will choose to rule beside me. I know it's customary, but still, I hate it.

I take one final look at the crashing waves before I turn, dragging my feet through the sand, I make my way up towards my mother. Her golden hair like mine sways in the wind, with a few strands catching the light more than others. She looks truly magnificent in her yellow sundress and I can see from the look on my father's face that he agrees. Even as we collect our belongings and enter the carriage, he doesn't stop staring at her.

"Can you please stop already? You sure know how to make me feel uncomfortable." I would have to be stupid not to understand the sexual tension brewing between them. It's disgusting. My mother's answering smile proves that I'm right.

"I can't help it; your Mother looks ravishing in that dress." My father smirks as he lounges back in his seat. He rakes his lust-filled eyes over my mother once more and I turn my head to look out the window. I only have to suffer through the carriage ride home, then I'll no longer have to endure this torture.

The thought of William looking at me, the same way my father looks at my mother, enters my mind. It sends butterflies swarming around in my stomach and the nerves from earlier rear their ugly head. I have dropped subtle hints for years about my growing feelings for him and he is either oblivious to my affections or he doesn't reciprocate them. I want to choose him tomorrow night. For him to be the one by my side through this life but how can I choose him, when I don't know how he feels? I desperately want him to choose me, the way I do him.

"Are you ready for tomorrow night, my dear, did the beach do the trick?" Mother asks.

"Unfortunately, no. I think I'm more nervous now than I was earlier today." I huff out a sigh as I slouch in my seat and cross my arms over my chest.

"Your nerves are normal dear. I wasn't excited about walking into a room full of men, all there to try and win my heart either. Thankfully, your Father whisked me away right at the beginning and fended off anyone else who came near me." She smiles at my father affectionately. The love between them is evident in their eyes.

"So, Father stole every other man's chance at getting to know you?" I raise an inquisitive eyebrow and stare at both of them.

"Ah, I wouldn't say that. Your Mother did speak to other men that night but she kept returning to me and I just didn't discourage her." Father rubs the back of his neck as he glances sheepishly over at my mother. Obviously, that was something no one else knows but them.

"What your Father says is true. He charmed me right from the beginning and for some silly reason I felt comfortable with him. Little did I know, that night, that I would fall madly in love with him and end up having you. It's hard to believe that you are now twenty-one and about to start your own journey of self-discovery. I hope you find a man that warms your heart and not just your bed."

"Mother!" I exclaim, shocked. Although I understand what she is speaking of, I was not prepared for her to say the words. Once I am wed, I know I must produce a female heir to carry on the family name. It is tradition that all titles fall to the firstborn daughter unless she chooses not to claim it. Then it would fall to the next in line. Unfortunately for me, I am an only child.

"Don't look so shocked dear, I only speak the truth." Mother leans over and lifts my chin, closing my mouth. I didn't even realise it was open. I nod slightly, sitting up in my seat as The Moss comes into view. My beautiful home is positioned on the edge of the Banks. The enchanted forest we do not dare venture into, without first offering payment to the magical beings that dwell beyond the border. I have heard about the nasty creatures that lie within its grasp. I myself have heard cackling when out for a walk along the tree line. It would be foolish to step into the forest without having your wits about you.

"You'll burn a hole through the trees if you look any harder." My father comments with a hint of amusement in his voice.

"Shh, you. Just go back to staring at my Mother, would you." I reprimand him half-heartedly and turn my gaze away from the Banks to stare towards my home.

"Don't mind if I do," he says playfully, to which I roll my eyes. My gosh, can we just be home already?

My pink dress is silky to the touch as I run my hands down the front of my skirts. My heart is hammering in my chest as I wait for them to announce my entrance. The sound of chatter filters through the closed doors and does nothing to calm my nerves. Deep breaths Jane, you've got this.

Suddenly, the doors before me swing wide open and Gerard, our butler glances my way. This is only for a moment and he gives me a small wink of encouragement, before turning back towards our guests. He clears his throat loudly and the room quietens almost instantly.

"It is my pleasure to introduce to you all, her Ladyship, Jane Hunterson." That is my cue. On shaky legs, I step over the threshold and into the brightly lit ballroom. I feel dozens of sets of eyes on me as I turn and begin to make my way down the stairs. I spot Ida, my best friend and her newly wedded husband Thomas, standing off to the side of the room. Her dark hair is half pinned up while the rest trails down the back of her gorgeous black gown. She clings to Thomas's tall frame with a beaming smile on her face as she watches me descend the stairs.

It was only last month that she was in this exact same position at her coming out party. She, however, almost stumbled her way down the stairs. I took the initiative and practised my descent many times over. I didn't want to make the same mistake she did.

My mother and father are waiting for me at the bottom of the stairs. My mother, as always, looks beautiful. Her hair is arranged high on her head so she can show off the magnificent golden jewel that hangs around her neck. She always likes to go a little bit extra for these events. I, on the other hand, have kept everything very simple. I am here tonight to choose a husband, not to sparkle brighter than the chandeliers overhead.

"You look radiant my dear." Mother places her hand on my arm and squeezes ever so slightly. Her touch calms my wayward thoughts just like it used to when I was a small child.

"There are a lot of men here tonight baby girl, try and speak to all of them if you can," my father says as he leans forward and kisses my forehead.

"I will try Father." I nod and take a deep breath in.

"Good. Now go and have fun. We will be around if you need us." Without waiting for a reply, they leave me standing by the stairs, walking through the throngs of people milling around to get a glimpse of me.

Ida rushes over and takes my hands within hers.

"Jane, who turned up the heat because it's hella hot in here? These bachelors are fine. How are you ever going to pick just one?" I cast my eyes around the room and capture a glimpse of shaggy brown hair. His strong jaw clenches as he smiles at the youthful brunette standing in front of him, his eyes crinkling in the corners. William. My stomach sinks at the sight of him conversing with another woman. She is wearing a sapphire blue gown that sparkles in the light of the room. Her long blonde locks are pinned back at the sides with flower clips made of jewels in the same colour as her dress.

"Tell me how you did it, Ida, how did you get Thomas to notice you?" I flick my gaze between William and my friend, shamelessly spying on his interaction with the beautiful woman. Ida turns her head to see who I keep staring at and lets out a little scoff.

"Oh Jane, you have it bad."

"Trust me, I know. He is all I have been able to think about since Father presented me with his damn list and I noticed William's name was on there. None of these other men mean anything to me, I don't know them like

I know William. He is all I want. I just wish I knew if he felt the same way, so I don't make a royal fool of myself. What if I choose him and he doesn't want me?"

A mischievous smile crosses Ida's lips.

"Then make him come to you. Let's find the most attractive guy off your Father's list and make William jealous. That's how I won Thomas after all." She boasts proudly.

"Ahh, I definitely recall that differently." Her smile falters as Thomas steps up to us from behind, handing Ida and myself a glass of champagne.

"Thank you." I graciously accept the glass and take a sip. The liquid is like heaven as it slides down my overly dry throat.

"Of course you would see it differently, but I know you were jealous." She whispers the last part as she toys with her glass. They lock eyes and appear to have a secret conversation that only they understand, which grows more heated with every passing second.

"Enough you two. Leave that for the bedroom." I chuckle uncomfortably as I move our little group away from the stairs and closer to the outer regions of the ballroom.

"Sorry, now where were we? Oh, that's right, we need to find you a hunky man to dance with." Ida takes a sip of her wine while gazing at the people around the room. She points to a few standing at the far left of the room but I shake my head. No, they won't do. I barely know them and the last thing I want to do is make awkward conversations with someone who may get the wrong idea. Gossip will spread like wildfire tonight, everyone betting on who I will choose based on who I spoke to. I nervously pull my bottom lip into my mouth when the sound of Williams's laughter rises above the chatter in the room. What in the world could they be talking about that's so funny?

I'm about to grab the first man I see and ask him to dance, just to take my mind off whatever they are talking about, when my eyes land on the perfect person. Standing in the middle of the crowd looking just as nervous as I, is Sir Noah Dashkov from the cross-over region. Although we are not close and have only spoken a handful of times, the conversations we have shared in the past have been pleasant and he has always offered a friendly smile. "What about him?" I whisper to Ida as I subtly point in Noah's direction. He is taller than most, making him stand well above most men his age. His brown hair is neatly combed to one side and his suit looks impeccably tailored to fit his tall frame.

"Ooooh good choice, he's gorgeous."

"Parden?" Thomas asks, giving Ida a questioning look.

"Oh shh, you know I have no eyes for anyone else but you. I am just being the supportive best friend that Jane needs me to be. You wouldn't want me shirking on my bestie duties, would you?" Thomas shakes his head with a smile breaking across his face, before walking off to join a group of men standing on the other side of the room. "Go ask him to dance." Without any warning she's pushing me towards Noah, not giving me a chance to change my mind.

I close the distance between us and stop less than five feet away. He's facing away from me, talking to the gentleman standing next to him. Noticing me standing there I offer him a polite smile and point to Noah. The gentleman kindly alerts Noah to my presence.

"Lady Jane, it's a pleasure to see you again." Noah straightens to his full height, placing his hands behind his back.

"The pleasure is all mine Sir Dashkov. I was wondering, would you do me the honour of dancing with me?" I sweep my hand in the direction of the dance floor and just catch the slight grimace that appears across his face in reaction to my question. Not the response I was hoping for. I pray to the gods that the smile on my face is pleasant and doesn't reflect the uncertainty I suddenly feel.

With relief, I don't have to wait too long for his response. "It would be my pleasure Lady Jane, but I must admit, I'm not a very good dancer. As a general rule I avoid the dance floor at all costs. I shall make an exception for only you and I apologise in advance for my clumsy feet." He says it with such honesty and sincerity that I laugh in reassurance. I thought he just didn't want to dance with me. What a relief!

Noah takes my hand and leads us onto the dance floor where a dozen or so other couples are already dancing. I catch my father's eye as I place my hand on Noah's shoulder and he offers me a small smile and wink over the rim of what I can only assume is an impeccably aged scotch in his tumbler glass. Clearly he approves of my choice in dance partner.

We dance through the remainder of the song currently being played by the string quartet with only minor toe stomping and conversation runs smoothly and with ease. We uncover that we actually have a lot in common and have a lot of the same goals and aspirations for our futures. I'm genuinely having an enjoyable time talking and dancing. Maybe Noah would make a befitting husband if William doesn't reciprocate my affections.

I'm laughing at something Noah just said, when I soon find he wasn't lying about his terrible dance moves. After a few spins and dips, Noah steps the wrong way, right on the top of my foot.

"Ouch!" I cry, wincing as I raise my foot off the ground. Pain has already begun to throb up my leg from my toes. That really hurts.

"I'm so sorry Jane. In my defence, I did try to warn you that I was a terrible dancer." Noah holds my arms to support me as I wobble on one foot while he looks around for help.

"It's ok, truly, I was adequately warned of the potential danger to my limbs prior to us taking the dancefloor. It is a simple accident. I just need to sit down." I try to offer him a comforting smile to appease the guilt I see in his eyes, but even I can hear the pain in my voice. I look around to see if I can catch the eye of a guard or attendant and notice we have attracted quite the attention. Almost everyone around us is staring at me. Well, this is just great, how mortifying. Here I was worried about gossip spreading over who I spoke with tonight and now all they will be talking about is how I hurt myself. I can only imagine the things they will be saying tomorrow in the square. Tears begin to well up in the corners of my eyes. This was not how this night was meant to play out.

Without warning a strong voice announces..."Here let me help," before I am suddenly lifted off my feet. Warm arms hold me securely to a wide muscular chest as I'm carried through the crowd. We are halfway across the ballroom when I look up into my favourite pair of smokey grey eyes. Our eyes stay connected for a few moments and I only break the connection to look back towards the dance floor, where I see Noah standing there watching us leave. If the situation wasn't so absurd, the perplexed look currently spread across his face would be comical. I offer him an apologetic smile before bringing my attention back to the man currently walking towards one of the ballroom's many exits.

"Are you for real? We're causing a scene," I whisper hiss, placing my hand on his chest with the intent to push him away. "Yes Jane, I am for real. You're hurt and in pain and Dashkov was just standing there like a bumbling idiot." I open my mouth to interject. Although Noah didn't take action, he did take the time to apologise for what happened. Before I can respond, William looks into my eyes, concern evident in his voice, "I will not see you in pain, when there is something I can do about it." My heart flutters and I move my hand from his chest, to rest on his face. His concerned eyes light up at my touch and he begins to smile.

William reaches the large ornate doors on the far side of the ballroom that lead through a hallway towards the kitchen. We make the walk to the kitchen in comfortable silence, William's declaration playing over and over in my head. Is his concern for me simply because we are the dearest of friends and he doesn't like seeing me hurt, or is it something more than that? The possibilities swirl around in my head and I barely notice we have reached the kitchen until I am ever so carefully placed on the benchtop. William makes his way to the freezer where he grabs some ice and wraps it up tightly in a thin cloth before returning to my side. Sitting the wrapped ice beside me on the bench, he gets down on one knee and lifts the front of my dress revealing my stilettos. "I need to take off your shoe to be able to assess your injury better, ok? Stop me if it hurts." We lock eyes for a quick moment and I nod my head in understanding.

He raises both hands to gently cradle my tender foot which is already starting to swell and begins to untie the pale pink ribbon that holds my heel in place. I wince as the pain intensifies the moment my foot is free.

William lets out a small whistle between his teeth as he takes in the sight of my foot which is already starting to turn purple. "Dashkov sure did a number on you." He's not kidding, my foot is on fire.

"It's definitely painful, more so now that my shoe is off."

"It is the release of pressure. You just had a lump of a man stand on your small delicate foot," he grumbles. Of course even in pain, William can still make me laugh. "A lump of a man? I would hardly call Noah a lump of a man." He looks up at me and I can see the chagrin in his gaze. "What kind of man doesn't know how to dance with a beautiful woman? Let alone risking hurting said beautiful woman." I pause in my response, trying to process what he has just said. Did he just call me beautiful? He has never called me beautiful before. I look off to the side, feeling the blush creep across my face. A sudden chill to the top of my foot brings my attention back to William and I see him holding the cold pack directly over the area that Noah stood on.

I wince at the cold and lingering pain. "This was seriously not how I pictured this night ending." I place my head in my hands, tired and ready for this night to be over. What a mess this night has become. Yes, I have the man of my dreams kneeling before me but he is only doing so because I got hurt. I am still going to need to get back out to the party somehow and put on a brave face for Mother and Father and choose my husband. It is required of me, there is no other option.

"Quite frankly neither did I." His words pull me back into the now and I lift my eyes away from my hands to look at him. The annoyed expression I expect to see on his face due to the inconvenience of the situation isn't there, instead, he looks happy. "I had a brilliant plan for how this evening was going to play out. I was going to wait until later this evening, once you had danced your way through all the lumps and halfwits who don't deserve you. I was going to then ask you to dance with me. I have always loved watching you dance. You're so graceful and radiate so much joy when you are whisked across the dancefloor. I wanted to share that moment with you in front of everyone, like we have shared so many other moments." I sit up straighter on the benchtop as he removes his hand from his pocket and produces a small object covered in a thin cloth. He gently takes the hand I currently have resting on my right knee and places the object into my open palm. "Happy Birthday Jane." With fingers shaking from nerves, I lift the material away from the object to reveal the most stunning brooch I have ever seen. The myriad of different shades of pink gems set into the delicate gold metal depicts a dahlia flower in full bloom. I have never seen anything so exquisite.

"Oh William," I whisper, shocked as I glance between him and the precious gift he has given me. "It's beautiful, thank you."

"While we were on the dance floor I wanted to present you with this gift. I wanted to declare my affections for you in front of the entire room and I wanted to take your hand as I have now and express my longing for you and tell you that your beauty and grace eclipses the exquisiteness of this brooch." I look into his mesmerising eyes and I'm shocked into silence. Is he saying what I think he is?

"I love you, Jane. I have for the longest time. Every smile, every laugh, every breath you take, has captivated me from the moment we met all those years ago. You stole my heart that day at the markets. You had chicken feathers in your hair and even then, I didn't think I had ever seen anything more beautiful. When I look at you my heart pounds. I want to wake up every day with you by my side, to love you and cherish you, grow old with you and always be together for the rest of our lives."

The sun beams down upon us through the large bay windows of my day room, warming the back of my exposed neck. Ida and I stand side by side as we sort through the swatches of material laid out on the table in front of us. I'm so giddy with excitement, in six days I will be marrying the love of my life. William is all I have ever wanted for so long and I can't wait until I can truly call him mine.

"Do you like pink or blue?" Ida asks, holding up two pieces of fabric. I barely spare them a glance before shaking my head. "Neither. I was hoping for a gold or white colour scheme, maybe even silver."

"Seriously, white?" Ida adjusts her focus from the fabrics to turn her blue gaze towards me and gives me a look, like I've gone mad.

"Yes, seriously. I think white would go nicely with the pink dahlia bouquets that will be in the centre of the tables."

"Of course you're going with the dahlias." Ida glances at the brooch pinned above my left breast and smiles. After William knocked me off my feet with his declaration of love that night, we shared the most perfect kiss. Not that I really have any experience with kissing. I shared an exceptionally unpleasant first kiss with Roman Northund who worked in the stables, not long before I met William. Back then I had a crush on Roman and would sit with him for hours while he cleaned out the stables.

I thought I loved him, now I know it was nothing but a passing infatuation and I can happily put that terrible kiss behind me. I can focus on the utterly magical kiss William and I shared and the love that I know without a doubt, that I feel for him. The night of my coming out party will forever be imprinted in my mind and cherished forever.

It wasn't long after our kiss that my mother and father came looking for me and found us hidden away in the kitchen, sitting side by side on the bench with my hand in his. I informed them that I had made my decision and that my wish was to marry William and that was that. My parents allowed William to assist me up to my wing of the estate, seeing as I couldn't put any weight on my foot. They then went back out to the party and announced to all our guests that I had chosen my future husband. They made apologies for my absence and William and I were able to spend a couple of uninterrupted hours together discussing our future and feelings for each other.

My parents are happy for us. Mother is claiming to have known all along, that we would end up together. I have my doubts on that one, how could she know something that I clearly didn't? It wasn't until William said the words, that I knew he loved me. Up until that point, I wasn't even sure he cared for me beyond that of friendship. My father just smiles with happiness every time the topic of our upcoming wedding is brought up in conversation.

I still don't think that I even believed it until the morning after the party. Ida showed up on my doorstep demanding I tell her everything that happened the night before and that's when everything really sunk in. I am going to be marrying William! Ida and I sat on my childhood bed, legs crossed and in my excitement the details poured out of me. I could see on her face that she was thrilled for me as well. We have only dreamed of this day since we were little girls and now all our wishes are coming true. She has already had her fairytale wedding and soon I shall have mine as well.

Focusing back on our conversation, I smile at Ida. "Would you mind heading over to the east wing and asking Suzy for swatches of the other colours, please? I'd like to test them against the silverware and napkins." I hold up the shiny new cutlery my mother ordered just for the wedding. They came all the way from Cambridge, the neighbouring kingdom.

"I'd tell you to go get them yourself but you're currently an invalid. It would be cruel of me to make you hobble all the way over to that side of the plantation. Plus, in your state, it would probably take you all day."

"Oh, do shut up," I wave my hand in Ida's direction, shooing her away. She turns to leave and laughs as she heads for the door. I shake my head as a smile crosses my lips. She's such a tease but I love her like a sister. Since my party, she has been giving me so much grief about getting my foot crushed by Noah. I can't believe it has been a little over three weeks and it still hurts to walk on. I'm on the mend though and I'm hoping I will be able to make it down the aisle without any issue. Unlike Ida, William on the other hand has been exceptionally helpful. He has been frequently checking in on me to see how I am going and making sure I am keeping off my injury. If it wasn't so endearing, it would almost be annoying how attentive he has been.

I'm in the process of putting away the pink and blue fabric swatches when the door behind me creaks. I don't need to look to know it's him. My body hums when he is near, tiny pin pricks of awareness running through my body. "How is the planning coming along, can we get married yet?" He asks, as he wraps his arms around me from behind.

I laugh at his ridiculousness. He has been asking me this every day since that night. "Not quite yet but it is going to be a truly amazing affair. Ida has just gone to retrieve some more colour options for the tables while I organise the centrepieces." I direct his attention towards the beautiful flower arrangement in the middle of the table. His grey eyes light up as he recognises the pink dahlias sitting in the ornate glass vase.

"Good choice." He whispers the words into my ear before he turns slightly to step in front of me and rakes his eyes over my body. His smile falters as he looks down and notices I'm standing on my sore foot. I know he and everyone else keeps telling me I need to stay off it so it can heal but I have way too much work to do. I can't just sit around all day twiddling my thumbs. "Not such a good choice, you should be resting it."

"I know, I just need to sort this stuff out and then I will." I turn around and lean my butt against the edge of the table. William drops down on one knee and without a word, lifts my leg and slides my shoe off my tender foot. The bruise on the ridge is barely noticeable anymore, only a slight touch of green is evident. It has healed up quite nicely, if only the residual pain would cease to exist. For the first two weeks after the incident, I couldn't even put pressure on it and I feared it may have been broken. Luckily though, I have been able to put pressure on it this past week and have even been able to walk on it in small doses.

"Jane, you should take better care of yourself. I would much rather have a downgraded wedding than a bride who won't be able to walk down the aisle." He stares into my eyes as he runs his thumb along the inside of my ankle. The sensation stirs something deep within me that I'm starting to become very familiar with and I forget to respond. I shift my focus to where he is caressing me and he notices my distraction, moving his fingers even higher up the inside of my leg.

My breath hitches when they reach my knee and William rises to stand before me. He holds my leg gently off the ground as he leans in close, his mouth brushing my ear. "Do you like this Jane?" He whispers softly before placing a tantalising kiss on the sensitive spot on my neck. He knows that spot drives me crazy. He has become very acquainted with that spot over the last three weeks. Stolen moments here and there that are so special to the both of us. I dare say that my mother would have a fit if she knew that I will not be a virgin on my wedding night. Since we declared our feelings for one another, we haven't been able to keep our hands to ourselves.

Our first time will forever be the most precious memory to me. William invited me out for a late picnic dinner under the stars. It was so romantic. He took me out to a quiet and secluded spot in the flower garden on the property. He had a rug with plush cushions and blankets laid out under the full moon and candles were lit all around the area. We shared a lovely meal together and one thing led to another. He was so careful and attentive that night, so cautious and an absolute gentleman.

A tickle to the inside of my knee brings me back to the present and I answer his question breathlessly, "Yes." William chuckles as he slides both hands along the backs of my legs until he reaches my ass. Like I weigh nothing at all, he lifts me onto the table. I carelessly shove a few things behind me out of the way and William pushes his hard length into my aching core. "Is this what you want Jane?" My body warms with need as my veins fill with a familiar fire.

I nod, not able to conjure a coherent thought before turning my attention to his belt. William chuckles as I quickly pull the soft leather through the loops and slide down his pants, setting him free. His length is impressive, well above what I've read it's supposed to be like in books. He lifts the skirt of my dress up to my waist and slides my panties to the side. "This is going to be quick Jane. Ida could be back at any moment." His warning comes seconds before he enters my body. We both moan in pleasure from the connection. There is nothing I love more than feeling him inside me.

My legs tighten around his torso, the urge to keep him cradled between my legs indescribable. He leans back a little and our eyes connect, the desire I see almost bringing me to orgasm. I raise my arms and grab him by the back of the neck, pulling his lips down to mine. "Move," I whisper, right before our lips connect. I kiss him hard and fast, wanting to taste every inch of his lips. I lick the seam of his mouth requesting access, right as he begins to shift inside me.

The pleasure builds deep within and butterflies swarm through my veins as they gravitate towards the apex between my thighs. My breathing turns heavy as William thrusts faster and faster, spurred on by my moans of pleasure. He trails kisses down the side of my neck as the table rocks beneath us, causing the centre pieces to topple over. My moans get louder as William moves his hands to my hips, his grip punishing. It is the best kind of pain.

His thrusts are desperate as he fucks me even harder. The sensations low in my belly intensify to a precipice and without warning, I explode, releasing myself all over his cock. In my euphoric state, I barely register William toppling over the edge and stilling deep within me. He's breathing hard as he rests his head on my shoulder trying to catch his breath.

"You, my darling Jane, are the most exquisite creature I have ever seen. Truly a sight to behold. I don't think I have ever seen anything more beautiful than watching you come." He says this through laboured breaths and we stay that way, with his head lowered and me rubbing circles on his back for only a moment before William lifts his head and places a sweet kiss on my lips. "I should go. Ida will be back any minute and you need to get back to wedding planning so that we can finally be married." At the mention of her name, my heart jumps into my throat and I swing my gaze to the door.

"Shit! I forgot about Ida. You need to leave. Now! Go through the side door. She won't see you if you go that way." I push on him hastily, just enough that he frees himself from my body. He starts to laugh as he pulls up his pants and without thought, I hop off the table and wince at the sudden pain in my foot. Ignoring it, I turn quickly to straighten the table behind me. It's such a mess.

"Am I a secret now, my love?" William asks with amusement lingering in his voice.

"Of course not, but I don't want her to know what we were just doing in here. One look at that smug smile on your face and she will have us figured out, before we can utter a word. Now go!" I point towards the side door, sparing him only the briefest glance and smile, before returning my gaze to the mess that is on the table.

"As you wish my lady," William chuckles but does as he's told. Thank the heavens. The sound of the side door clicks shut just as the entrance doors open. I scramble to tidy the remaining fallen centrepiece as Ida walks through.

"Suzy was not pleased that you asked for more swatches. I had to listen to her drone on and on while she searched for them. Apparently, she has more important things to do for this wedding than search for more fabrics." Ida says this as she stops at my side and hands me the three pieces of cloth. I take them from her as she inspects the table in front of us with scrutiny, her gaze shooting to mine. "Hang on a second. You're flushed. Your forehead is spotted with sweat and why is the table covered in water and fallen flower petals? Something's going on here." She looks around the space before her eyes stop on the only other exit in the room.

I can tell the exact moment she figures out what is going on. Her eyes whip towards me, the biggest grin I have ever seen spread across her face. "Oh you're naughty, definitely naughty." She nudges me with her shoulder, a salacious look in her eyes. "Shut up. Don't act like you and Thomas weren't fornicating all over the place before you got married. You are no saint my dear Ida". She laughs as she glances down at the table next to us. "We are no longer working in here." Ida gathers up as much of the contents from the table as she can and heads for the door. "Grab the flowers and meet me in your room. Or have you done it there too?"

"Not yet," I mutter. Ida smiles and just as she is about to leave the room, she says... "Good because you might want to change when we get there, your ass is wet." Her laughing can be heard as she walks down the hall and I swing my head around to look at the back of my dress. She's right, it's wet. It must be from the water we spilt all over the table. Damn it, I don't want to get changed. The scent of William's aftershave clings to my dress and I want to keep it there. Exhaling a breath, I pick up the remaining items and make my way out of the room. I don't even care that we were busted by Ida, I don't regret what we did. How can I regret something that feels so unbelievably right?

A storm is brewing in my stomach and I get the odd feeling like I'm going to throw up. Breathe Jane... In... Two... Three... Out... Two... Three... It's no big deal. You just have to walk into that room, in front of all those people, whom you have met many times before. You've got this. I nod to myself as I repeat those words on loop in my head, pacing in front of the doors that lead into the chapel.

"You look absolutely stunning, my darling girl," my father proclaims as he descends the stairs into the grand lobby. His tuxedo is neatly pressed and he's wearing the pink bowtie I requested for the occasion. The heels on his boots click against the marble floor as he makes his way over to me.

"Thank you Father, you don't look so bad yourself." I reach over and straighten his bowtie which is hanging just a little too much to the left. Now it's perfect.

"Are you ready to go in?" He asks and the guards standing by the doors straighten in readiness. He moves to stand by my side and I link my arm through his. My dahlia brooch catches the sunlight streaming in through the windows high above, bringing a smile to my face. William is waiting for me on the other side of these doors.

"Absolutely." I smile and nod to Samuel, the guard on my right, who lightly taps on the door, notifying the herald on the other side that I am ready. The sound of a harp begins to play, followed by a violin and then the rest of the string quartet.

Frederick, the guard on my left, smiles as he opens the doors into the chapel and all eyes are on me. This, this is what I was so nervous about. Having everyone look at me as I walk down the aisle. This is so much harder than walking into a ballroom for a party. I thought choosing my husband was the hard part. Oh Gosh, if there are any angels watching over me, please don't let me fall.

"Breathe Jane," my father whispers as we take our first steps into the room. At his words, I realise I'm holding my breath. I look down the aisle and on the other side of the room I see William waiting for me. My love. I smile and take a calming breath. I forget about all the other people in the room as butterflies swarm in my stomach at the sight of him. He looks like a dream, one that I have been longing for, for as long as I can remember. His black suit is a stark contrast to the whiteness of the room. His hair is neatly combed back and he is wearing the pink tie I gave him yesterday. He is the reason I am here today, to become his wife. Nothing else matters.

I see a tear slide down the side of his face as he stares at me but he's quick to wipe it away. His eyes never stray from mine as we make our way down the aisle. William's smile grows wider when we step up to the altar and my father reaches forward to shake his hand.

"She is all yours my boy." He grips my soon-to-be husband's hand before leaning forward to hug him. My father whispers something into his ear which makes William laugh.

"Thank you, sir," he says, with laughter in his voice as he takes my hand and we turn towards the priest. William glances my way and our eyes lock and I wish I could pause this moment. To remember how truly happy I am, that I have found my soulmate. My own true love to stand by my side through this life.

"You are so beautiful." He smiles at me as the priest clears his throat. I mouth the words thank you from under my veil and we both turn to face the man who will make us husband and wife.

"In the name of the Holy Spirit. Dearly beloved, you have come together in the presence of us all, to share your union with one another." The priest glances out at the crowd behind us before looking down at the book in his hands.

"William Mickelson and Jane Hunterson, have you come here to enter into marriage without coercion, freely and wholeheartedly?" The priest looks up from his book and looks at us both.

"I have," William says, before I also respond in agreement.

"Are you prepared, as you follow the path of marriage, to love and honour each other for as long as you both shall live?"

"I am," William confirms and turns his beautiful eyes to me. "I am," I say as I stare back at him. His smile grows wider with every declaration we make.

"Since it is your intention to enter the covenant of Holy Matrimony, join your right hands and declare your consent before the Holy Spirit." William and I turn towards each other and I reach for him. He takes my hand and I give his a little squeeze, while his thumb rubs gentle circles along the back of my palm. He offers me a small wink before taking a breath.

"I, William Mickelson, take you, Jane Hunterson, to be my wife. I promise to be faithful to you always. Be your protector through the good times and the bad. I will be the shoulder you lean on when you get sick and will always be there when you need someone to ice your clumsy feet." Everyone laughs at this; he knows it wasn't my fault but his declaration warms me. "I vow to love you and honour you all the days of my life, from this day forward." I see my mother out of my peripheral vision wiping the corner of her eye with a handkerchief. She needs to quit that right now if I am to get through my own vows.

Giving my full attention to William, I take a deep breath and speak from the heart. "I, Jane Hunterson, take you, William Mickelson, to be my husband. You are the only man I ever wish to have by my side, through this life and beyond. I will always be faithful to you and take care of you when you cannot do it for yourself. I shall be your sounding board and always make time for you, no matter how busy things may get. If you ever find yourself in need of assistance to wrangle up the chickens again, I'm your girl." Only those that are close to the both of us laugh, most in attendance not knowing how we met all those years ago, but the chuckle and sparkle in William's eye tells me I made the right choice in adding that in. I smile up at him as a tear starts to slide down my cheek and I almost choke on the last part. "I vow to give you all that I am. My heart will forever belong to you." William uses the hand that isn't holding mine to reach up and gently wipe away my tears. His other hand holds mine gently but firmly, silently giving me his strength.

"May the spirit in his kindness strengthen the consent you have declared before your family, friends and the kingdom.... Oh, Holy Spirit bless these rings, which we bless in your name. So that those who wear them may remain entirely faithful to each other, abide in peace and in your will, and live always in mutual charity." The priest dunks the rings in a bowl of holy water beside him, slightly drying them off before handing them to each of us.

"William, please place the ring on Jane's finger and repeat after me......Jane Hunterson, receive this ring as a sign of my love and fidelity. In the name of the Holy Spirit." William repeats the words and slides the plain gold band on as requested. Once it's on, he looks up at me and smiles.

"Jane, if you could please do the same.... William Mickelson, receive this ring as a sign of my love and fidelity. In the name of the Holy Spirit." I do as instructed, getting the ring stuck as I push it over his knuckle. The priest chuckles as he watches my struggle and once it's finally secured in place announces, "In the sight of the Holy Spirit and these witnesses, I now pronounce you husband and wife! You may now seal this union with a kiss." The entire room erupts into a flurry of cheers as I smile up at William, laughter on my lips. I can't believe it, we're married!

"Finally," William breathes, raising my veil over my head. Without breaking eye contact, he cups both sides of my face in his warm hands and leans in close. He seals his lips gently over mine. The kiss is soft and sweet, I can tell he is holding himself back by the way his hands hold my face. He is conscious of our audience and who is watching. If we were alone, I have no doubt that he would be ravishing me right now. We have barely been able to keep our hands to ourselves, but now that we are married, the feelings have intensified. Tomorrow we leave for Enchanted Cove and I cannot wait. Three full weeks alone, with my husband, uninterrupted, at my favourite place in the world. We can do whatever the hell we want to each other then. What more could a woman want?

The sun kisses my skin creating a luscious warmth through my body. I'm in absolute heaven right now. William is spread out on the lounger beside me with a book in hand. He's reading about faraway lands with dragons and knights, the tale of two brothers fighting for the love of one woman. I read the book years ago and found it to be extraordinary.

"I can't believe it, so after everything Derek did for Rebecca, she still chose Luke. It's a horrible story." William closes the book and tosses it onto the table beside him. He crosses his arms and stares out at the rolling waves, crashing into the shore. He is too cute right now, grumpy over the outcome of the story.

"You're obviously missing the point, my love. It's not about how many people he killed for her, it's about where her heart lay in the end. Yes, Luke was penniless but that didn't matter to Rebecca, she still loved him anyway." I sit up on my elbows and follow his gaze out to sea. Seagulls fly high overhead on the lookout for their next meal. The sun is starting to set on another glorious day, the skies above are a wondrous mix of pink and yellow. My eyes catch sight of some small clouds that linger just above where we lay on the beach and I get lost staring up at them.

"Have I told you today how beautiful you are?" William questions, bringing me out of my thoughts. I turn to him and see his eyes locked on mine. He adjusts his body to fully face me, giving me a spectacular view of his chiselled chest. What a specimen he is. "Come for a swim with me." He doesn't wait for a response, before getting to his feet and walking off towards the water. The muscles in his back strain with every move he makes which causes my insides to flutter. We made love this morning as we bathed and I haven't been able to stop thinking about it since.

I quickly get to my feet and race off down the beach towards him. I catch up just as his toes touch the cool water, with the intention of jumping on his back. He surprises me though and spins around and catches me. Pulling me close he seals my mouth with his, walking us deeper into the ocean. He grins against my mouth, the icy water making me yelp as it touches my tender nipples. I wrap my legs tighter around his waist and drape my arms over his shoulders. Once we are neck-deep in the chilly water, Williams's hands find their way into my hair.

He slightly tugs the long strands, directing my face away from his and unlocking our lips. Trailing kisses up the side of my face towards my ear he whispers, "I want you." I can feel his length pressing into me.

"So, what are you waiting for then?" I tease. I barely get the words out before William's lips crash into mine. I lick the seam of his mouth, wordlessly seeking more and he eagerly lets me in. His tongue is warm and soft as it greedily massages mine. I shamelessly moan into the embrace.

Without breaking the kiss, William untangles his left-hand from my hair to free his well-endowed cock, while his other hand finds its way to tightly grip my ass. Without pause, he pushes my swimmer bottoms to the side, positions himself at my opening and guides my pussy down until I'm seated to the hilt, his shaft buried deep inside me. My breath hitches in my throat at the sheer size of him. The fullness is an excruciating burn that I cannot get enough of.

"Fuck! You're so tight," he groans as he begins to slowly thrust in and out of me. Warmth floods my veins and I meet him thrust for thrust, tension building in the pit of my stomach, aching to be released. My breaths are laboured as the heat builds within me and I reach up to cradle the back of William's head, to bring his lips back to mine. I kiss him like my life depends on it and my walls tighten around him as my body builds towards its climax. Reading my body and impending release, William grips my ass tighter and thrusts his hips harder into mine. Our bodies crash together, William forcing my body faster against his, creating waves in the water around our bodies. I feel him start to tense under my fingertips and I know he is close.

"I need you to come baby," he growls, his warm breath tickling the side of my face, causing me to shiver.

"Only if you come with me." I tilt his head to the side and start trailing kisses down his cheek. My body bounces at a rapid pace but I continue until I reach the crook of his neck. I swipe my tongue directly over the spot where his neck meets his shoulder, tickling the sensitive area, right before I bite down gently over the same spot. I know exactly what it does to him and it takes only a second before his thrusts become uneven. I feel him swell within me and that, combined with the sensations already building up inside me, tip me over the edge. An orgasm like I've never felt before rips through me and I barely register the guttural roar that William releases out to sea. I'm spent and if it wasn't for William holding me securely against him, I would float out with the tide.

"That was sneaky, my love." He's breathless, his heavy inhalations matching my own as he pulls out of me gently and rests his forehead against mine. We stay like this for a moment until we are both recovered from our love making.

"I've gotta keep a few tricks up my sleeve." I offer him a mischievous smile and without giving him any warning, break out of his hold and dive under the waves. I swim a distance away, swimming closer to the shore and when I am certain I am far enough from where I left him, I break through the surface. Turning towards the direction I just came from; I wipe the water from my eyes and open them to meet William's smokey grey ones. "You want to play baby?" The smirk that pulls across his face and the gravelly tone of his voice sends tingles through my body. He only just gave me a mind blowing release and I can already feel the heat building inside me once more. Tilting his head to the side I watch his eyes darken right before he commands, "Run."

I squeal and make a break for the shore, pushing my legs to run faster as the water slows me down. I can hear him slicing through the waves behind me as I continue to laugh, my heart pounding with excitement. I know he will catch me; he is so much faster than I am, but the chase is exhilarating and I love this playful side of him. My feet barely touch the sand before his strong arms wrap around me and he tackles me to the ground, ensuring that I land on top of him. Our chests heave with exertion and laughter as we look into each other's eyes, the smile on William's face is more beautiful than the sun setting behind us. "You caught me," I laugh.

His arms tighten around me, holding me closer in his embrace. "Baby, I will chase you to the ends of the Earth. There is no place I won't follow you." He leans forward and presses his lips to mine. This kiss is full of love and promise. I taste the salt water on his lips and the kiss increases in intensity. William's hands are just sliding down my body to grab my ass when a wave crashes to the shore spraying up over our bodies.

I shriek in surprise and try to push off William's chest to get out of the way, but he holds me securely against him. His warm hands grasp me firmly by the waist, keeping me in place and I glare down at him while he chuckles. "Don't give me that look baby, you were already wet.......... from the water.... and from me." The salacious smirk that crosses his smug face makes me laugh.

"Oh my god, William! I can't believe you said that." He rolls us over so that my back rests against the wet sand and manoeuvres his body to lay between my legs.

Looking down at me he says, "Making you wet is my second most favourite thing in this world." I exhale on a shallow breath and question, "And what is your most favourite thing?" The hand resting on my hip slowly slides up my body and just as he reaches my ribs, says, "Making you laugh."

He proceeds to tickle me in all the places he knows I'm ticklish and I giggle and squirm trying to get away. We roll in the sand for a few moments together and when we eventually stop to catch our breaths, I close my eyes and thank the stars that this is my life. I know this is only our honeymoon and it won't always be like this. I have a duty to uphold when we get back home but knowing that William is my husband and will be by my side to give me stolen moments like this along the way, makes me warm inside.

"I have a surprise for you." He whispers quietly and I open my eyes to look at him. He is smiling from ear to ear and I can't help but smile back.

"You do?" My heart beats with excitement.

"Mmhm, but first we need to wash off all of this sand and get changed." I bite my lip as he gets to his feet and holds out a hand to pull me up. Once I'm standing, he releases me and heads towards where we left our towels. I stare at his retreating back, watching the muscles move as he walks and I wonder what the surprise could be. "Are you coming or what?" He calls out over his shoulder. I shake myself out of my thoughts and race after him. I guess I won't find out waiting out here, so I better catch up.

Earlier, after leaving the warm soft sand of the beach, we made it back to our room in record time. We both managed to shower while keeping our hands to ourselves and William instructed me to dress in something nice. Naturally, I went for my favourite gold, floor length evening gown. It swishes around my ankles as we walk hand in hand down the stone footpath that leads back towards the water. Maybe my surprise is an evening under the stars.

My dahlia brooch sits proudly above my left breast and it twinkles in the fiery light of the lanterns that light our way. Since William gifted it to me all those nights ago, I rarely go anywhere without it. I chose the sandals I'm wearing tonight purely for the reason that the pale pink crystals match my brooch beautifully. As we make our way onto the sand I reach down and unclasp my shoes wanting to feel the sand in between my toes.

It's cool to the touch and I savour the feel of it. There is nothing like this back home and who knows when we will have the time to come back here for a visit. When we return home, I will take over from my mother and my duties will ensure that I am left with very little down time. We won't be able to escape to the beach as often as I would like.

"This way my love," William says, pulling me to the left and down further along the beach. In the distance a dozen or so lanterns have been assembled in the shape of a circle around an elaborate table with a white lace tablecloth. As we get closer, I notice that the table is set for four. My brows knit together as I look up at my husband and see him smiling down at me.

"Are we expecting someone?"

"Did you really think that we wouldn't come help you guys celebrate?" A familiar feminine voice calls from behind me. I whirl around to see my best friend and her husband standing only a few feet away. My jaw drops at the sight of them and I turn my wide eyes towards William.

"Well, it wouldn't be our honeymoon without celebrating it with our closest friends now, would it?" His happiness is evident as he raises his hand and closes my mouth. "Don't look so shocked my love," he laughs as he leans forward and steals a kiss.

"Sorry," I smile happily, shaking my head. "I ah, I can't believe this. Oh my gosh. You guys are here!" A small tear of pure joy slides down the side of my face as I let go of my husband and run over to embrace my friends. Ida gets to me first, wrapping her arms around me and Thomas joins in by hugging us both from the side. I laugh at his antics and exclaim, "It's so good to see you both."

"Oh my god Jane, it feels like it has been forever! I need to know everything. I want to know all about what you two naughty kids have been up to, shacked up here, all on your own." She offers me a mischievous little wink and I blush, but before I can respond we are interrupted.

"Dinner is served," one of the senior waitstaff calls from the table. We slowly make our way over and I grab a hold of William's hand and squeeze it tight. I can't believe he planned for them to come here. We both cherish their friendship so much and to have them here with us is the best thing in the world.

"So William, now that we are here, what have you got planned for us?" Ida asks, taking her seat opposite him at the table. I grab my napkin from my plate and place it on my lap and look over at my husband as a sexy smirk appears across his face.

"Oh Ida, you're impatient as always." William smiles with devilish intent as he stares across the table. I can tell he's getting a kick out of toying with her. I grin as my eyes go back and forth between the two of them. I look at Thomas and he rolls his eyes, making me laugh. We're both used to their bickering antics.

Ida doesn't back down as she waves his comment away and retorts, "That I am, so are you going to tell us or what?" She tilts her head to the side and drums her fingers along the table, giving an air of mock impatience. They stare at each other for a moment and William shakes his head.

"Not yet," he says, giving her a sly wink as he leans back in his chair. "I'm starving, let's eat."

"I may be impatient William, but you sir are insufferable."

"Don't I know it." William chuckles as a waiter lifts the cover from the plate in front of him, revealing the most delicious pasta I've ever smelt. My stomach grumbles at the sight of the creamy goodness.

"Oh my, that smells amazing," I mutter as the waiter moves behind me and reveals my meal. Another waiter on Ida and Thomas's side of the table follows suit and we all stare in excitement at the food in front of us. William picks up his wine glass and raises it for a toast.

"To the greatest of friends and the sexiest wives. Thank you both for coming to celebrate this wonderful occasion with us. Let's all raise our glasses, drink and have fun! Cheers." A blush creeps over my cheeks and I feel Ida's eyes on me. I glance over at her as I raise my glass and clink it against the others before taking a sip.

She has this look on her face that spells trouble and I just know she is up to something.

"I wonder, just how much fun will we be having William?" Ida tries again to coax him into telling her his plans.

"You're just going to have to wait and see Ida," William retorts, not giving her a lick of information. I giggle, shaking my head. Ida won't drop it until she knows every small little detail about her trip here. She is not the kind of person who likes surprises. Just being the surprise, apparently.

"Well, if you're not going to tell me what your plans are for while we are here, can you at least tell me what you have planned for after dinner?" Ida lifts her fork from the table and starts digging into her meal. "I think that's something you will need to discuss with your husband Ida. I have plans with my beautiful wife and they certainly don't involve you." William smiles at Ida as he takes a sip of his wine before placing the glass back on the table.

"William!" I exclaim. I'm not a prude by any means, but does he really need to discuss such things in front of everyone? The waitstaff are standing close by for goodness sake. Thomas chuckles but doesn't say anything. I think he is having too much fun watching them bicker to be concerned with impolite dinner conversation.

"Don't worry so much darling. We are husband and wife; everyone knows what we get up to. Plus, how can I be expected to keep my hands to myself when I am married to such a beautiful woman like yourself?" William looks my way and smirks. Oh good Lord, please open your gates and swallow me whole. My body feels hot from the blush that creeps over my skin. I choose to ignore his comments, bringing my attention back to my plate and take another bite of my dinner. The flavours of mushrooms and bacon mixed with garlic and cream explode on my tongue. It's absolutely delicious.

"Leave my girl alone, would you?" Ida playfully glares and points her fork at William. She gives me a sidelong smile and I realise she's trying to change the subject. That's my girl, she's always got my back, just like when we were kids.

"Never going to happen. I will not apologise for wanting to worship the love of my life. The very reason for my continual existence. I'm afraid she's stuck with me." William shrugs his shoulders unrepentant. I stare at him, lost for words. How do you respond to that? He looks over at me with a gentle smile and raises his glass to his lips once more.

"This meal is delicious, William. I must get the recipe to give to our chef." Thomas breaks the silence that has come over the table. A smile creeps onto my lips as I look up and see him looking at me before he turns his head towards William. Yep, Thomas has my back too.

"I must agree Thomas, the chef has certainly outdone himself. I'll ask him to pass on his recipe." William and Thomas continue their discussion while Ida and I continue to eat our meal. The stars shine brightly above us and I marvel at the wondrous sight. There are so many constellations, way too many for one person to count in just one night.

"So lovebirds, what have you guys been up to so far?" Ida enquires during a lull in the conversation. I look to William as I smile and say, "Oh, just a little bit of this and a little bit of that. Sunbaking and swimming, enjoying each other's company." He looks over at me shaking his head, a playful grin spreading across his face. I know he is thinking about earlier today when we rolled around in the sand.

"You surely are an inquisitive one tonight, aren't you Ida?" He leans back in his chair, resting his arm over the back of mine. The warmth of his skin seeping into me as it brushes against my neck. "I'm just trying to make conversation Billy boy.... so, what little bits of this and that are we referring to... hmmm?" Ida's eyes sparkle with glee knowing just how much Willaim hates being called Bill. She used to tease him about it all the time when the old ladies in town called him that.

It is for this exact reason that Ida used that name. She knows it will get to him and he won't back down from the provocation.

William rakes his hand through his shaggy brown hair and leans forward, resting his elbows on the table. He stares at my best friend, the challenge evident within his eyes. "Well, if you want to know that badly Ida, I'll tell you." William glances sideways at me and I have the sinking feeling that I am not going to like what he has to say.

"Don't," I warn, flicking my eyes over to the waiters standing not too far away.

Ignoring me, William continues, "As Jane said, we've gone swimming and done a spot of sunbaking, we went hiking a few times and even kicked back and had a couples massage together." He finishes speaking and I take a relieved breath, that was nowhere near as bad as I thought it would be. William has a knack for oversharing and I have a feeling that is exactly what Ida was hoping for. Usually it doesn't bother me but tonight we have an audience and our staff do not need to hear what we have been getting up to. However, before Ida can formulate a response William continues, "Oh, and I've also had her up against a tree, in our bed multiple times, on the sand and as of today even in the ocean. Is that the sort of gossip you were after Ida?" And there it is. The intimate details of our life are now out there for all the staff to gossip about.

Ida chokes on her food, clearly not expecting for that to come out of William's mouth. Even though she likes to rib and tease him, she knows that this is not the place to speak of such things. He laughs at Ida's reaction and glances towards me but I just shake my head. "If you'll please excuse me. I think I'm done for this evening." I wipe the corners of my mouth with my napkin and stand. Without another word I turn away from the table and begin to head back to our villa. William calls my name but I ignore him and continue walking up the beach that leads to the paved path. I can't believe he was so careless with something so private.

"Jane, please wait." William catches up to me and grasps my arm, turning me to face him.

My body feels hot. At this point I am unsure if it is from embarrassment or anger.

"No William, you shouldn't have said what you did. I don't care if Thomas and Ida know, they are our friends and lord knows they certainly don't censor anything around us, but you spoke about special moments, private moments that you and I have shared together in front of our staff."

"I'm sorry my love, I didn't think."

"No, you didn't and what has upset me the most is those special moments are now tainted because every time I think of them, I will be wondering if the staff are whispering amongst themselves about it. I know you were trying to be funny and Ida certainly knows how to get under your skin, but I am about to take over the rule of these lands and its people. I understand this is something that you have never had to think of before but for me, this has always been a part of my life. I will always be the favourite topic of gossip and you just handed them the loaded gun. You need to be conscious of what you say and in what company. If it was just the four of us, then it wouldn't have been an issue, please just be mindful of what you say in front of who, moving forward." I pause and take a breath, needing to take a moment to calm down.

I know he isn't used to having to think about these things and he didn't mean any harm. I really wouldn't have had an issue if it was just the four of us. "I'm done for this evening. Please wish them both a good night for me. I'm going to bed." I turn and continue towards the path and I can feel William's eyes on me as I walk away. For all the distress built up within me at this moment, I say let him look. We have never really fought before, but this is the first dispute we have had since we declared our love for one another. It has caused a sick feeling in the pit of my stomach and I can only hope that in future he thinks before he speaks in front of such company.

The sun shines through the open window as the curtains move back and forth on the early morning breeze. My husband sleeps soundly beside me while lying on his stomach. I watch his back rise and fall with every breath he takes and I hate the fact that we had our first real disagreement last night. My mother once told me that arguments are healthy in a relationship. She said that a relationship consists of two people with two different personalities who have their own opinions. Arguments facilitate a space for couples to build a greater understanding of each other, develop trust and forge an unbreakable bond between them. We are bound to disagree at one point or another.

I was asleep when he got back last night. I didn't even feel him climb into bed. I may have slightly overreacted about the events of the previous evening but I really want to start my reign off on the right foot. I don't want there to be rumours or gossip being spread about me.

I sit up and rub the sleep from my eyes before stretching my arms above my head. It's going to be a beautiful day. I wonder what William has planned? He stirs slightly beside me and I hold my breath as he rolls over. My heart beats slightly faster than normal as his eyelids flicker open and his mesmerising grey eyes connect with mine.

"Hey beautiful," he mutters tentatively. Sitting up next to me, resting his back against the headboard, he watches me.

"Hey," I whisper. The uncertainty in the air is suffocating as I try to think of what else to say. He turns his eyes away from mine and gazes at his empty hands resting on the bed. We sit there in silence for far too long before I can't stand the tension any longer and blurt out, "I'm sorry about last night. I see now that I may have overreacted to the whole situation." I turn away from him to look out the window beside the bed. The palms sway in the warm gentle wind and I can hear birds off in the distance enjoying the new day. The bed shifts as William reaches over and takes my hand in his, bringing my attention back to him.

"No, I'm sorry my love. I was so excited that they were here and I got a little carried away with the banter between Ida and I. I'm so sorry that I didn't consider the ramifications of talking around the staff and I have already had words with both servers that were waiting on us last night. They have assured me that they will not speak a word of what they heard. Plus, I know who they are now so if anything comes out, I will know where it came from. I hurt you and made you feel uncomfortable and Jane, I am so incredibly sorry. That wasn't my intention at all. I never want to be the cause of any suffering that may befall you. I want to be the one that supports you and has your back through the tough times." He brings my hand up to his lips and gives my knuckles a gentle kiss. "Please forgive me?" He asks softly. His eyes search mine as he waits for my reply and I can only nod in response, my throat tight from unshed tears.

He breathes a sigh of relief and cups my cheeks in his large callused hands, bringing my face up to meet his. Our lips connect in the softest of touches. This kiss isn't about passion and the burning desire we share for one another, but reaffirming our love and commitment to each other, no matter what. A single tear slides down my cheek and William breaks the kiss to wipe it away.

With a small smile William says, "Now that we have resolved that, are you ready to have some fun?" The unsure man from a moment ago is gone and in his place is what can only be described as a kid at Christmas, ready and waiting to receive his presents.

"Are you going to tell me what you have planned?"

"Nope. Just get dressed in something comfortable and meet me outside for breakfast." He leans over and kisses my forehead before climbing out of bed. He makes his way into the bathroom and shuts the door behind him. Putting the events of last night behind me I throw back the covers and quickly dash over to the closet on the far wall. I am filled with excitement knowing he has planned a whole day of fun for all of us. I rummage through my belongings looking for something pretty that fits the comfortable directive I have been given. Do I even own such a thing? I eye a pair of khaki pants folded neatly on the bottom shelf and question if they would be suitable. They would definitely be comfortable. Hoping I have made the right choice I slide them on and do up the fly and then grab a plain black loose fitting top from its hanger and slip it over my head.

I have just finished tying the bow embellishment at my neck when William opens the bathroom door and steps out, fully clothed. His gaze roams my body, the heat in his eyes making me feel like I'm not wearing anything at all.

"Good choice, I'm proud of you darling. I was expecting to walk out here and find you sitting amongst a pile of silks and chiffon," he comments before smiling widely at me.

"Well I certainly didn't get any assistance from you my dear husband. Wear something comfortable, he says. I'll have you know that even the highest pair of my heels are pleasant to walk in." I poke my tongue at him cheekily and turn back to the cupboard to find some footwear for the day.

He makes his way over to the bed laughing at my words and leans down to grab his own shoes from the floor. "No heels today my love. Please find something a little more sturdy." He walks out of the room through the bi-fold doors and out onto the terrace. Muffled voices float in from outside and I would recognise those high pitch tones anywhere, Ida. Wanting to apologise to the others for my poor behaviour last night, I grab my black trainers from the shoe rack and put them on. I dash into the bathroom to fix my hair, brushing out the ends and tying it up into a high ponytail. Even up, my golden locks still hang halfway down my back. I look at my reflection one more time in the mirror, making sure I look ok, before I walk out of the room to join my husband and our friends for breakfast.

"William! Stop teasing. Just tell me what we are doing today." As I step outside I see Ida playfully shove William in the shoulder. He chuckles and her pouty face immediately softens the moment she notices me standing there.

"Morning Ida." I take the empty chair beside my friend. Thomas must still be getting ready as it's only the three of us seated at the table.

"Good morning Jane. I'm really sorry about last night. I went too far and I didn't consider the company we were in. As soon as you left, I realised my mistake and why you were so upset. I would never willingly put you in such a situation, I was merely enjoying the playful teasing of my best friends and I let our banter get the better of me. Can you find it in your heart to forgive me?" She reaches across the table and places her hand on top of mine.

I turn my palm over under hers to grasp her fingers firmly and an embarrassed smile breaks out across my face. "You're already forgiven. I agree you pushed it too far but I also over reacted. It's just that there is going to be so much attention on me when we return home and the last thing I want is for people to be talking about private moments that William and I have shared. I want them to talk about how well I lead my people and the things that I achieve in my reign."

"I have no doubt that you will do the most amazing things, my dear Jane." She gives my hand a final squeeze before I direct my attention to William. "Now that that is settled, will my darling husband here tell us what we are doing today?" William currently sits relaxed in his chair, a glass of orange juice in one hand and spinning his sunglasses around with the other. He hasn't said a word since I sat at the table and I know he was giving Ida and I the space to make amends. Before William can respond I notice Thomas approaching the table in my peripheral. He takes the remaining seat on Ida's other side while greeting us all and William just looks around the table at us and winks, he raises his glass to his lips and takes a sip. "Oh, you guys are in for a treat."

Our horses' hooves pound against the sand as we race each other along the beach. The pace is far more exhilarating than our previous activity. After finishing breakfast William led us down to the garden where we played croquet. We spent the morning enjoying each other's company and ribbing one another. It was filled with lots of laughs and Thomas decimated the game by getting the ball through all 6 hoop points first and even landed the peg in the middle on his first try. Ida came in a close second but ended up fumbling on the sixth hoop. She claimed there was a bee buzzing nearby which distracted her. I'm not sure if I believe her though, Ida has always been a sore loser. Regardless, it was a really great start to the day.

But nothing compares to riding Prince. His mane flies in the midday wind as we gallop along the shore. William is in front of me by a hair's breadth and sand from his horse kicks up in my face. I spit the grains out of my mouth while I wipe the rest away from my cheek. I'm closing in on him and thank the heavens because I'm exhausted. We have been galloping at high speeds for well over thirty minutes. My poor boy has done an amazing job and is going to need a well needed rest after this. He currently has a sheen of sweat along his coat.

I dig my heels into Prince's side, encouraging him to go just a little faster. I can see the finish line, it's just over a hundred metres away and at this point it's between William and I, on who will be the winner. William glances behind him to look over at me and laughs. The cheeky ass thinks he's going to win. He should know better; he knows I'm the better rider and he just made a crucial error taking his eyes off the end goal.

"Get him Jane!" Ida yells out behind us. Thomas and Ida stopped trying to compete with us a few hundred metres back, they know this is a competition they are not going to win. Focusing back on the finishing line I raise myself slightly out of my saddle giving Prince more room to move. With less weight on his back legs, he kicks up in speed and we come up beside William and his stallion. The shock on his face would make me laugh in any other situation, he was certain he would win this challenge but

I keep my eyes on the prize and I smile when we surpass him and cross the finish line before them.

"YES!" I cry out as Ida and Thomas cheer behind us. I pull back on the reins, slowing Prince down to a trot, gently bringing him down from the fast pace. He is a beautiful horse, such a pleasure to ride. He moved when I needed him to, sped up when encouraged and even now, absolutely exhausted, he is following all of my commands.

"Show off!" Ida calls and I pull on the reins, steering us over to the others. We come up alongside Thomas's brown stallion and I dismount. I rub along the side of Prince's white neck in thanks for the most amazing ride. William walks over to me placing a gentle kiss on my forehead and whispers "Congratulations, my love."

"He was magnificent, darling. I've never ridden a horse like him."

"I'm glad you think so because he's yours." My eyes shoot to his in question.

"Mine?"

"Yes my love, yours. I bought him as a wedding gift for you. I know how much you have missed riding since losing Blazer and I wanted you to be able to have your own horse to ride again." I squeal in excitement and wrap my arms around his neck, pulling his lips down to mine. I kiss him until a discreet cough reminds me of where we are.

"Thank you, William," I whisper breathlessly, as a single tear slides down the side of my face. How did I get so lucky to have this man to call my own?

"You are most welcome, Jane." He leans forward and kisses me ever so softly. Ida clears her throat again and we unlock lips to look over at her.

"Sorry to break up this little love fest but are we doing anything out this way or are we heading back to the cove? I personally don't want to be around if you two are about to get hot and heavy, if you know what I mean." Ida shudders and William flips her his middle finger. We all laugh at her comments, but I can feel a slight blush creep up my neck. Some alone time doesn't sound like a bad idea.

"As a matter of fact, Mrs bratty pants, you *are* needed down this way. I have arranged afternoon tea for you ladies up on the ridge." William points past the horses and shrubbery up to a table shaded by a huge umbrella. I lift my head and gaze at the beautiful space he has arranged for us. He really has thought of everything. With the coming out party and then the wedding, Ida and I haven't really spent much time together.

"Thomas and I will spend some time fishing off the pier. Who knows we might even catch our dinner." My nose screws up at the thought of fresh fish making William laugh. "Or not. Either way, off you go ladies. We will see you a little bit later."

William leans forward, placing a sweet gentle kiss on my lips before stepping away. "Have fun... Come on Tommy boy, the last one to catch a fish has to do a nudie run after sundown." William grins from ear to ear as he sprints towards the pier. "Cheating prick!" Thomas yells after him. He swifty kisses Ida goodbye before chasing William along the sand. Ida links her arm with mine as we watch our husbands push and shove each other, both attempting to tackle the other into the sand.

"Men! Or should I say boys? They act like bloody children." Ida shakes her head as we turn and make our way towards the table set up on the ridge. "And what, we don't?" I ask, raising my brows. I don't think I've ever seen anyone throw a tantrum quite like Ida.

"We do, just not when the men are around." She flashes me one of her mischievous grins as we trod up the hill. On the grass landing a beautiful table is spread out with the finest of china and cutlery, glasses of champagne and orange juice lay before us. "Your man thinks of everything," she remarks, as we come to a stop beside the table.

Approaching from a tent set up not too far away a waiter greets us and pulls out our chairs for us to sit. It's warm today and the sun shining down on us, topped with the race along the beach by horseback, has me parched. I raise the glass containing the orange juice to my lips and drink the entire thing in a matter of seconds.

"Thirsty are we?" Ida gazes at the empty glass in my hand.

"I think racing William up the beach really did a number on me," I mutter, placing the glass on the table. The waiter comes over and refills it before returning to her station. She fiddles with a few latches on her cart before opening a door, revealing a four tier cake stand. She carefully pulls it off the shelf, walks over and places it in the middle of the table.

"Well this certainly looks yummy." Ida stares at the array of food set out before us. "Where do we start?" She questions, looking over at me. Although my stomach rumbles with hunger, I shrug my shoulders, I'm beginning to feel a little off. I think I overdid it during the ride.

"Maybe we begin at the bottom and work our way up?" Ida begins to reach for the food without waiting for a reply. Everything smells heavenly and it takes me a moment to select a few options before putting them on my plate. Taking a bite of hash brown, I moan, it's soft and almost melts on my tongue the moment I put it in my mouth.

"Mmm, that is so good," I groan around another bite. The waves crash against the shore not too far in the distance and I can't help but marvel at the tranquillity of the afternoon. Can it always be like this? It's peaceful and relaxing and nothing at all like back home. I huff out a sigh, collapsing back in my chair.

"Hey, are you ok?" Ida questions. I can hear the concern in her voice.

"I was just thinking about home. I have had such an amazing time here these past couple of weeks and the thought of returning to the Moss to assume control from my mother has me feeling anxious. I am to be responsible for all of our people. What if I'm not ready, Ida?"

"You were born ready Jane. You are going to rule this land with a firm but gentle grace. You will show compassion when it is deserved and be inflexible and strong when you need to be. I know it, William knows it, hell the whole of Mossidaria knows it. You are going to be an amazing ruler."

"But what if I can't be what everyone needs?"

"That's not even possible. You and I both know you won't ever let someone down. For if there is even an inkling that you may, you will kick your own ass to ensure you get the job done. And if that doesn't work, I'll be right there to kick your ass for you." Ida vows as she bites into her bacon. A small smirk appears in the corner of my mouth at her words.

"You always know how to reassure me, thank you for being such an amazing friend?" I reach over and hold her hand briefly in mine before returning my attention to my own bacon.

"I've got your back babe. Always."

We are quiet for a few moments, focussing on our food and enjoying the afternoon sun. There is a light breeze in the air, scents of the ocean travelling up to us where we sit on the hill. Grabbing a slice of cherry pie from the stand between us, Ida breaks the silence to ask, "Have you had any thought into what your first proclamation as ruler will be?"

"I want to plant fresh produce along the streets within the Moss. Different varieties, so no matter what the season is there will always be something for those less fortunate to eat." The memory of a homeless woman I once saw in the town square comes to mind and I will never forget the look on her face as I gazed upon her. So much sadness built up deep within her blue eyes. It was the only time I ever felt shame for being who I am, but I vowed that day that I would make a difference. I will feed the hungry and shelter the poor. I will ensure medical supplies are readily available to those who have none. My mother helped the less fortunate in other ways. She was of the belief that everyone is entitled to an education and has done an amazing job getting children off the streets and into classrooms. I, in no way, disagree with the work she has done. It warms my heart to see the children working hard in class every day, I just believe we need to support the more basic needs first.

"Jane, that's an amazing idea! Have you told William?"

"He has already started making a list of the different fruits we can plant and where to plant them." I smile as I glance at the array of deserts before me. I eye a lemon tart on the third shelf and place it on my plate before cutting off a piece and placing it into my mouth. The moment the citrusy sugar hits my tongue I groan internally. Delicious.

Ida smiles over at me. "Of course he has."

"He loves the idea. He's already been down to some areas of Mossidaria that I'm not allowed to venture to without an escort and he told me that there is a lot of homelessness down there. Can you imagine it, Ida?" Tears well up in my eyes before one escapes down the side of my face. "This is only the first project for William and I. We plan to spend our ruling making the quality of life better for the homeless population."

Ida is silent as she stares off into the distance. I have no doubt she is picturing the numerous times we have walked the streets and seen the desolate faces of the unfortunate. "I'll be right there with you Jane. This project is going to save lives, I just know it. If there is anything you need just let me know, okay?" The love I have for this woman and her unwavering support is beyond description.

"Thank you Ida. I couldn't imagine having it any other way." I raise my glass of champagne towards her and she lifts hers to clink with mine.

"Girl, I will support you in all your dreams and do anything I can to help you achieve them. Well...almost anything. Do you remember that time you wanted weed roots that bordered The Banks?" A chuckle escapes my lips as I nod. "You were definitely on your own with that one. There was no way in hell I was getting that close to the enhanced woods without an offering. You were living on the edge that day."

"Oh come on! I didn't even get that close. You're just a scaredy cat." I lean back in my chair as my stomach starts to feel icky again. Maybe I've just had a tad too much sun. The weather is awfully warm and I have spent the entire day outside.

"Scaredy cat my ass. You got so close that anything could have grabbed you and pulled you in. I almost died just watching you." Ida's eyes go wide as she recalls that afternoon, years ago. It is not common for folk to walk so close to the forest wall, but I have been doing it for as long as I can remember. Though, my mother would have had my hide if she knew. In all the years I have lived next to the woods I have not once seen any of the creatures that live within.

"Yep, as I said, scaredy cat." I mutter under my breath. I smile over at her as I take a sip of champagne, the bubbles tickling my tongue as I swallow.

"No, it's because I have more common sense than you do." She raises her brows with an air of superiority and I can't help but laugh.

"You, seriously? I call bullshit!" I sit up straight and rest my hands on the table. We wouldn't have gotten into half as much trouble as we did when we were younger if it weren't for Ida. She has always been the instigator out of the two of us.

"Call it as you will but I know the truth." She shrugs her shoulders.

A strong gust of wind blows suddenly from the south, knocking the umbrella completely out of its stand. Before we have a chance to get up and stop it, the umbrella gets blown further along the ridge and out of reach. The red headed waiter indicates for us to stay and she quickly chases after it. We watch her for a few minutes as she struggles to catch it, but I'm suddenly pulled away from the poor girl when Ida asks, "Have you and William spoken about children yet?"

"What?" I choke out, staring straight at her. Where in the world did that come from?

"Kids, Jane. Have you guys spoken about it yet?"

"Sheesh Ida, we only just got married. Children haven't even crossed my mind yet. Can't I at least get through my honeymoon first?... What about you, have you guys talked about having kids?"

"Thomas and I have spoken about it briefly. He wants to wait a little before we bring rugrats into this world. I quote, 'I want you all to myself for a while before we have kids that restrict our sexy time.' Like a child would make me any less adventurous. It would probably do the opposite if I'm being perfectly honest. I can't wait to be a mum; I'm gonna rock that shit."

"I couldn't agree more. A child would be such a blessing. To have a little me or William running around, getting up to mischief and annoying the kitchen hands just like we used to." The vision of a grey eyed, brown headed baby plays in my mind, bringing a smile to my face.

"You would make the most amazing mother Jane. You are so kind and compassionate. Any child would be lucky to have you as their mother."

"And an aunt like you." I offer her a gentle smile. She is going to be the most spectacular mother. Her love for life and adventure will build the stepping stones that ensure her children grow up with the same enthusiasm and passion in anything they do.

Trying to conceal the moisture in her eyes, Ida looks out over the water. We sit here in companionable silence for a while enjoying the peace and serenity the afternoon has brought us. After about fifteen minutes or so, Ida breaks the quiet, "I think I see the boys returning from their fishing expedition. Should we head down the beach and see if there are any fruits from their labour?"

"Absolutely, though I certainly hope there aren't any. I am not eating any fish that they may have caught for dinner." We laugh as we push out of our chairs and get to our feet. I swipe the glass of water from the table and quickly down it as Ida comes to stand by my side. I really think I have just had too much sun today, hopefully hydrating will make me feel better. I loop my arm through Ida's and we continue our joking over the terror of them cooking us fish for dinner. We laugh in earnest as we begin to make our way down towards the beach and our men.

My heels click against the marble flooring as I make my way across the grand foyer of our Moss residence. My mind has been in an absolute haze since we returned from our honeymoon a little over a week ago. From the moment I stepped out of the carriage, Mother whisked me away and put me straight to work. I've walked every inch of this estate fifty times over that my legs ache and I've signed endless requests, decrees and so many nonsensical documents that my hand is throbbing. Nothing can diminish though, the happiness and warmth I felt yesterday watching the first seedlings being planted in the newly ploughed field down by the old water mill.

As promised, the first decree under my reign to receive my signature was for fruit and vegetable gardens to be planted in any available fertile soil throughout my territory. On the day the decree was signed, the chatter that went through town reached all the way to the estate. By the end of the day there wasn't a single soul that resided within Mossidaria, that didn't know what I had proclaimed. I could tell that the people were sceptical. These types of things take time to implement but unbeknownst to everyone else, I have been working on this project for years. I already had a team picked out to prepare the ground and plant the trees and seedlings; I already had a rough idea on where these sources of food would be planted and with William's assistance, we were able to locate over five other locations that worked perfectly for our needs. I have been planning this project for a very long time, waiting for the day I could make it happen.

It has all been worth it too, the looks on the faces of the disadvantaged when a team of men started to prepare the overgrown grassland near the mill, that very next day, was an emotional one to say the least. From then, I have received an overwhelming amount of support from not only the general townsfolk but from those that are less fortunate. Whom have offered to care for the growing plants and ensure they are watered regularly. I cannot describe how humbled I am to know that everyone supports something I have spent tireless hours on. All this hard work has taken its toll on me though and I'm drained. The effects of the exhaustion are starting to wear on me and I know I need to rest or I'm going to burn myself out.

Lost in my thoughts, I'm startled by William walking through the front doors. "There you are my love. I haven't seen you all morning." He approaches and wraps his arms around me and places a gentle kiss on my forehead. The heat of his skin seeps into mine and I sigh for the calmness he brings. Except for the moments we have shared late at night in our bed, it seems like we haven't had a second to ourselves since we got back. The only times during the day have been at breakfast, dinner and when we are working on the gardens project. While I have been working tirelessly with my mother, William has been working alongside my father to learn the role that he will play ruling by my side.

"Are you ok sweetheart?" He pulls back a little to look into my eyes, I know the evidence of my tiredness is clear across my face. I'm sure he can see the dark circles that have gotten increasingly darker over the last few days. It doesn't matter how hard I have worked during the day, nor how exhausted William has left me after our lovemaking in the evenings, I am still having difficulty sleeping once twilight falls. My nights are riddled with restlessness and I'm struggling to feel refreshed in the morning.

"Yes and no. I'm finished for the day, which means there is no one demanding my attention or needing me for anything. Thankfully, because I am utterly exhausted and I've been feeling rather off the last few days. I'm sure I just need rest but that is easier said than done at the moment." I place my hand over my abdomen as a wave of nausea washes over me.

"Darling, you should head up to our room and lie-down seeing as you have no further commitments this afternoon. Take the opportunity to get some sleep. I could call for the doctor while you rest and wake you once they arrive?" William asks, with concern clear in his voice.

"A doctor isn't necessary my love." I bring my hand up to his face and caress the stubble across his cheek. "I might go for a walk in the gardens for a bit, the fresh air usually makes me feel better and then I might head up for a nap after that. Care to join me?"

"As much as I would love nothing more, unfortunately I can't. Your father has requested help moving furniture out of a room on the second floor. He needs all the muscle he can get." William smirks, flexing his arm beside us.

I laugh at his childish antics. "Fine, run along then. If you finish early, you know where to find me." I reach up on my tippy toes and place a gentle kiss upon his lips.

"I will surely come find you, if I am so lucky. Enjoy your walk my love, I'll see you a little bit later." He grasps my hand and places a lingering kiss to my skin before making his way towards the east corridor of the estate. I watch him walk away for a minute, then make my way to the large oak front doors and walk out into the fresh spring air.

The afternoon sun is warm on my skin as the slight breeze blows my hair away from my face and I can smell the floral scents of the orange, pink and red tulips that border the estate. I make my way through the grounds and I can see my staff rushing around the courtyard trying to get everything ready for the grand soiree I have arranged for tomorrow evening. I have invited Grandessa's nobility back to The Moss in the hope that they will wish to help fund my garden project. I have done the maths and I know I can fund the majority of the work I would like to achieve but with their help, we will be able to take this objective further and hopefully spread it out past the borders of Mossidaria. Our country could thrive with their assistance and what joy it would bring, knowing we were a part of it.

Enjoying the quiet, I make my way past the main gates and down towards the open fields. The ground is soft beneath my feet and I run my hand through the knee length foliage. The blades of grass prickling my palms brings back memories of Ida and I running through these exact fields when we were kids. Our fathers would play with us for hours down here until our mothers told us it was time to come in. I laugh out loud at the tantrums we would pitch when they wouldn't let us have more time.

I breathe heavily, loving the feel of the clean air in my lungs. It feels like forever since I was able to step away from the confines of the estate and out into the open. My stomach continues to feel a little unsettled and I rub it, to try to soothe the discomfort as I make my way over to the unmarked trail that runs alongside the Banks.

The woods are exceptionally quiet today except for the few birds I hear chirping far up in the trees. I look to the left and see my home. It is a massive three story structure that looms over everything else around it. It's an intimidating site.

"You should be more careful walking this close to the Banks in your condition." I halt mid-step, my stomach dropping. The warning didn't come from along the path behind me but from within the dense forest to my right. I swallow hard as I swing my gaze in the direction that I heard the voice and see a woman standing there just past the barrier. She is absolutely stunning with the palest white skin I have ever seen. I can make out the flecks of gold within her emerald irises and her long wavy red hair peeks out under the edges of her black hooded cloak. She lifts her arm and with long black talons, flicks her hair out of her face. Her unwavering stare ensnares me and I am frozen in place. This is the first time I've ever encountered a witch. Well any creature who resides in the forest for that matter.

Usually we never see the creatures that dwell beyond the barrier line. If we have the need to travel through the woods, we present our offerings to the inhabitants the night before. If they accept our request, the gifts are gone by morning. If they decline, well, let's just say you know you're not welcome; but you never ever see the creatures within.

"I... I'm sorry... Wh... What condition?" I stumble over my words.

"You're pregnant, Jane. Walking this close is not safe for you. Many creatures within these trees would take you and your unborn child for a snack. Leave here, go back to your pretty home of brick and glass and be with your husband." Seemingly done with her demands, the witch gathers her cloak and prepares to step back into the trees.

I'm pregnant? I place a hand over my stomach, tears of happiness welling up in my eyes. I'm going to be a mother! I can't wait to tell William.

Just as the witch is about to enter the thick foliage, I desperately ask, "Are you sure... that I am pregnant?"

The witch looks back over at me with a sad smile. "Yes, Jane. I am sure. You are currently growing the first Hunterson baby within your womb." Her eyes glance down at my stomach for a moment before she lifts them to meet mine.

"So... does that mean I will have more than one child? How do you know such things?" I have so many questions I wish to ask but can barely formulate the words to speak.

"I cannot give you the answers you desire, little one but I'll be seeing you soon, my dear." She spares me one last glance before turning and walking away.

I'm left bewildered by her parting words and shocked into silence. Getting my bearings I quickly recover and yell out, "Wait, what do you mean I will be seeing you soon? I don't understand." Confusion and happiness fight for dominance within me and I try to process the events of the last five minutes.

The sadness that was present on the witch's face and her strange parting words are soon forgotten though, as I stand there cradling my belly. Will our child be smart and courageous like their father, or quiet and calculating like me? Will they have William's brown hair or my blonde curls? I absently rub my stomach, loving the knowledge that there is a little life growing inside me and suddenly recall the witch's warning. Walking near the Banks is not safe. Cautiously, my eyes search the forest for any sign of danger but I see, nor hear nothing. I know they are out there though and that is enough of an incentive for me to leave. If the witch took the time to warn me, then I should heed her advice.

I glance over my shoulder towards The Moss. There is one person inside those walls who is going to be overjoyed about the news I have. My heart lights up with glee as I turn and sprint back up the grassy path, my exhaustion from the last week now out of mind. I may be the ruler of Mossidaria and have the weight of that role on my shoulders, but who knows what tomorrow will bring and I know with the love of my life and this baby beside me, I can do anything.

The End!

The Dahlia

FOLLOW KRISTEN

~ 2 ~

I would love to hear from you!

You would seriously make my day if you got in
contact with me on my social media pages.

You can find me on Facebook – Author Kristen
Dovnik. I'm on here quiet regularly.

I'm also on Instagram – authorkristendovnik
I'm frequently on here.

And for those of you who do not have social media
you can find me at my website. www.kristendovnik.com

I hope to hear from you soon
X

KRISTEN'S AUTHOR BIO

Kristen loves to write just as much as she loves to read. For years, she's imagined wonderful characters and exciting storylines, just waiting, waiting to be brought to life. Now that her children are a little older, she has the time to enjoy her passion for writing and is putting pen to paper, giving life to her characters and stories.

Kristen resides in Sydney, Australia with her husband Robby, and three very energetic, young children. She loves nothing more than spending time with her family or sitting down with a slice of vegemite toast, a good cup of coffee and writing the next exciting chapter for her characters.

Secrets
OF The
Dahlia

PROLOGUE

"Hello my darling, here, let me tuck you in," My mother says with a smile on her face as she walks into my chamber.

"Thank you," I reply quietly. It's not very often that my mother has the time to wish me a good night. She is usually busy with her duties as Queen, though she always makes time where she can for me. "Are you ready for tomorrow?" I ask as she takes a seat beside me on the bed. She leans forward and tucks a stray hair behind my ear, her skin smells like roses and peppermint lollies, ones I sneak whenever I'm in her office.

"Madeline darling, do you understand what is happening tomorrow?" My mother questions as she gazes upon me seriously. Without replying I shake my head. "Your father and I are going to make an announcement. We will be putting an end to a law that will affect your future in particular."

"What do you mean?"

"You are not aware of this yet as we did not want to burden you, like it did me. But there is a law that states that you as the future heir, must marry nobility on or before your twenty-first birthday to assume the throne.

Your father and I recently visited every noble man and women within the regions to request they sign a declaration, demolishing the law. We want you to have the opportunity to marry whoever, whenever you want and not to be forced to take a husband just so you may become Queen. I was lucky years ago that your father turned out to be royalty, otherwise I would have been forced to marry a man your grandfather's choosing." My mother smiles and I can tell she is thinking of a long ago memory, yet I'm confused at her comment.

"I don't understand." I state as I sit up a little higher on the bed.

"I think it is time you know how your father and I met, let me tell you the story. Almost eight years ago...

"Your Royal Highness," a semi older man proclaims as he drops into a short bow in front of me. "It's such a pleasure to make your acquaintance. Please allow me to introduce myself, I am Duke Firebreather of the

Crossover region and this is my nephew, Viscount Firebreather," the duke states as he gestures to a much younger man standing behind him.

"Your Highness," mutters the young Viscount as he too sweeps himself into a low bow. He is quite handsome for a man around my own age. It's such a shame he doesn't interest me at all, I didn't miss him greedily eyeing off my jewellery when he walked in earlier. I don't think he will be staying long.

"Gentleman please, the pleasure is all mine," I reply sweetly as I give them a pleasant smile. I'm perched on the edge of my seat at the end of the throne room wishing I could be anywhere else but here. I'm really getting tired of this.

At the end of the month I will turn eighteen and the law states that I must marry and take my rightful place as Queen of Grandessa. My father the current King has gathered every eligible suitor within our kingdom.

As the reigning King it would usually be up to him to decide who would be a suitable partner to stand by my side and rule as an equal. However, my father is allowing me to choose. His only request is that I meet with each one individually to get to know them first and then send the ones I don't like home.

I have been sitting here all morning listening to introductions, thankfully there are only two left. I *would send them all home today if I could because I've already found my King. The only problem is, he isn't of royal blood. This means I have no other option and the men must stay until I make a choice, otherwise my father will do it for me.*

Trying not to show my disinterest I address the gentleman in front of me, "I hope your stay in Millasea will be to your liking. Our lackeys will show you to your rooms. I'll meet with you in the gardens this afternoon Lord Firebreather, but for now if you will please excuse me. It's been a very long morning. I bid you farewell gentlemen." I leave no room for argument as I get up and curtsey before heading towards the side door. Although I'm tired, there will be no rest for me. I need to go see Ashton down in the stables. I need some of the comfort he brings, especially if I am to endure another afternoon of listening to potential husbands drone on about how great we will be together.

My ladies maids stand to attention the moment I step into my chamber. On the table beside them are the few clothes I will need to conduct a swift wardrobe change. They know my plans and know exactly where I'm going, it has been my daily routine for the past three months. My mornings are occupied with royal duties, I spend midday with my love and then it's back to the drudgery for the afternoon.

My maids have warned me from the beginning what will happen if my father finds out that I'm involved with a commoner, and not just any commoner but a marksman for a rival Kings army. I know the risks I'm taking to be with him, yet I try to ignore them.

From the moment I was born, my mother and father have been grooming me to rule. Not once have I ever done anything for myself. This is my only chance to truly be happy, everything will be different once I take the throne.

"He's not waiting for you down in the stables today Your Highness, but at the top of the clocktower," Sally whispers quietly as she helps me change.

"The clocktower?" I ask in astonishment. We always meet in the stables and take the horses out for a ride in the countryside. Lingering around the castle too long is risky and there is a high possibility of being seen.

"Yes, Your Highness. He sent word earlier," she says while stepping away to fetch my shoes.

"Very well, thank you Sally," I say in appreciation. They are endangering their own lives by helping me, but I know that even if I ordered them to leave they wouldn't because they have been caring for me since I was a child. I have come to love them like aunts and not as just maids.

"You're welcome Your Highness." Sally slides on my shoes and then moves to stand by the door. Rachel conducts a few little touch-ups to my hair before she too moves away to stand by Sally's side. I give myself a quick once over in the mirror and nod my head in approval, I could be mistaken for one of my maids. These ladies are magnificent at their job.

"We must leave now Your Highness, the guards shift change is almost over." Rachel bounces from one foot to the other as she reminds me of the time.

"Sorry you're right, let's go." I head towards them and out the door.

The three of us rush through the labyrinth of hallways underneath the main staircase until we reach the door leading out into the alleyway behind the castle. The moment I cross over the threshold my ladies turn back the way they came, they will cover for me if anyone asks where I am.

No one notices me as I rush past them on my way to the clocktower. It is located in the centre of Millasea and the marketplace is flowing with patrons as the lunchtime bells ring from high above. Gazing up at the tower from below I notice a glimmer of black sitting in the window and I pick up my pace. Ashton. There are hundreds of steps within the centre of the tower and I practically run up them all.

"Ashton?" I call out breathlessly as I reach the top and peer around the giant bell. He is standing off to the left gazing out the window, looking over the city with his hands stuffed into his pockets. He turns, hearing his name and as our eyes connect, his beautiful green ones piercing and bright shine as the most loving smile I have ever seen spreads across his face.

"There you are my love. I was beginning to think you weren't going to make it," he says as I hastily walk over to him. Ashton removes his hands from his pockets and places them upon my hips, pulling me forward and into his loving embrace.

"Why are we meeting here instead of at the stables, aren't you afraid we'll get caught?" I question, as he places a sweet kiss upon my lips. Ashton is wearing his uniform which identifies him as someone not of this land but that of an adversary and my father would see it as treason if I were found, as I am now with Ashton. It is not fully understood why there is so much tension and combatants between our lands, all my father has said is that it started before he was born. I don't think he even knows why.

"Yes and no, I just... I can't stay long. I'm sorry to say this my love but King Johnson retracted the brigade, so we're heading home today," he replies with sadness lingering in his voice.

"What?... You said the King wanted you to stay until the Princess chose a husband." I gasp as I'm suddenly overcome with sorrow. This can't be happening. Tears fill my eyes and I feel like I'm on the brink of hyperventilating.

"Shhh darling, it will be alright." He pulls me into a tight hug. "Originally we were only meant to be here until our business was concluded, it was only by luck that we were given this extra time, but last night he sent word and requested that the Prince return home." Ashton leans back with me in his arms and we gaze into each other's eyes. I can see by the look on his face that he is also struggling with what is happening and has no desire to leave.

"But you can't leave Ashton... I love you," I whisper as tears begin to slide down my face.

"And I you, Rosie. If the choice was up to me I would stay and never leave your side, but I swore an oath when I joined the brigade. I swore that I wouldn't abandon them and I am a man of my word."

"What about us?" Agony like I've never felt before tears me apart, while I gaze into Ashton's loving green eyes.

"I will come back for you. I will find a way to be free from under the King's hand and we will leave this place forever." A single tear slides down his cheek as he leans *forward and kisses me. His kiss communicates all the love in his heart and I wrap my arms around his neck, holding him close, never wanting this moment to end. I knew this day would come, I just didn't expect it to be so soon.*

Ashton has been in my every thought for the past three months and in a matter of hours, he will be gone. My life will return to nothing but fulfilling my duties as the future Queen. There will be no love or blinding passion, only the dull grey hue of living with a husband I did not wish for.

"You promise?" I stupidly ask when he moves his mouth away from mine. It will make no difference if Ashton did return, I will be engaged or even married by then. My father will have chosen a suiter and I will have no choice but to do as I am told. So even though I don't want to, I know I must say my goodbyes.

"I promise," he declares honestly as he pulls me closer and I rest my head upon his chest. We stand there within each others embrace, the crowds below unaware of the pain coursing through me. After a while he grabs my chin and lifts my lips to his, his kiss is gentle and full of love. My heart is breaking and I have to remind myself to keep breathing. You will heal, it might just take some time.

Ashton pulls away with tears lingering in his eyes and he whispers, "I love you," before placing a gentle kiss upon my forehead. "I will see you again," he promises as he turns and heads for the stairs.

For a few seconds I don't move. I stand there stunned, not quite believing what is happening. I'm gazing upon his retreating back, he is taking my heart with him and I don't know if I'll ever get it back.

Just as he is about to descend the stairs, Ashton looks up and blows me a kiss. I mouth the words, "I love you" and see him smile, before disappearing into the darkness. I drop to my knees on the hardwood floor and sob into my hands. Will there ever be any light in the world, now that Ashton's gone?

It's been three weeks since the events that took place at the clock tower, three weeks since I've been able to feel anything but sadness. I have turned away every possible suitor as I can't even stomach the thought of spending my life with anyone but Ashton. My father is disappointed that I could not make a choice on my own and it's now up to him to choose for me as my birthday is less than a week away.

It's a tradition here in Grandessa, that the new King and Queen be welcomed at a ball held in their honour, *on the Queen's twenty first birthday. I may not have chosen who my future husband will be but my mother has faith that my father will find someone in time. She is so confident in this, that she has been working tirelessly around the clock to plan the lavish event by herself. I have been of no help in the matter, I just cannot bring myself to care.*

My brothers got to marry at whatever age they wanted and to whoever they wanted. In Grandessa it is the female who is the heir, which meant they had no restrictions, where I am forced to take a life companion at the ripe young age of 21. This law is so stupid. Why should I be excited to marry someone not of my own choosing, just so I may take the throne? I should be able to choose.

We are two days out from the grand ball and my father believes he's found a suitable man for me, although my mother doesn't approve. They have been bickering all evening at the end of the dining table, but I've tried to ignore them, it's not very often that they both can agree on something. He is Lord somebody or other from a neighbouring estate, but my father feels it's a satisfactory match.

Suddenly there is a small commotion by the side door as a messenger hastily walks in and abruptly stops by my father's side. "I beg your pardon, Your Majesty. King Johnson has announced himself and is waiting for you in the throne room." My father gives the messenger a baffled look before he nods and waves the messenger away.

"What do you think he wants?" I ask hesitantly before taking a sip of wine. Could the King have found out about Ashton and me? No, he couldn't have, surely not. Though, what if he did? Oh god I'm done for... Except, I used a fake name. Ashton didn't even know the real me.

My hand slightly shakes as I place my glass back upon the table. Everyone in the dining room is completely silent while my mother and father discuss what to do next. I watch their heated discussion before both sets of eyes turn towards me.

"I do not know, but you're coming with me," my father announces as he gets to his feet and heads towards the side door. "This will be a great learning opportunity for you." I'm still trying to process his words through my anxiety, when he halts mid-step. Before entering the hallway, he turns and gives me an impatient look and as quickly as I can, I rise from my seat and rush over to him. I link my arm through his and we begin walking silently through the corridors,

down towards the throne room. We stop just outside the door and I feel my heart beating erratically in my chest as my father turns to me.

"You will wait here and listen to the proceedings through the door, understood?" I'm about to argue but he gives me a look that indicates this is clearly not the time for dispute.

"Yes, father." I bow my head and watch as he nods to the guards and they escort him in. The moment the wooden doors close, I move to place my ear against it.

"Fillis, what are you doing in my Kingdom?" My father booms and I hear his heavy footsteps, as he makes his way to sit upon his throne.

"It's so nice to see you too, Howard," King Johnson states with amusement in his voice.

"Cut the chit chat, what do you want?" My father responds, I roll my eyes. My father secretly loves verbally sparring with King Johnson.

"Well then, I'll get right to it. A little birdy told me that your daughter has turned away every potential suitor within your kingdom."

"And that is your business why?" My father will give nothing away.

"Because I believe I have a solution for you." He answers candidly.

"Is that so?" I can hear the scepticism in my father's voice. Although I also detect intrigue. Maybe my father isn't as happy with his current choice of suiter, as he had me believe.

"Yes. As you may know, my youngest son Ames has recently married. My eldest Theodore has yet to marry and I believe that if these two were to wed, we could potentially end our father's ridiculous feud and finally become allies," Johnson proclaims with great determination. I'm shocked at his words. Our two kingdoms have been at war since before my father was born. Surely he won't agree to this.

"I'm guessing that's why you're here then?" I'm confused by my father's question, when suddenly a new voice responds, "Yes, Your Majesty."

"Hmm...," he murmurs before calling out my name. "Cordelia?" For a second I'm motionless as the doors swing open before me. He cannot seriously be considering this. "Cordelia!" He calls out again impatiently and I know I'm making him look bad. I shake myself out of my stupor and rush into the throne room, heading straight for my father's side. Without lifting my head, I drop myself into a half curtsy out of respect for the King of Cambridge and then lift my eyes to the men before me.

My heart skips a beat as I gaze upon the Prince. He has beautiful tanned skin and shaggy brown hair and *although he isn't as tall as my father, he is tall, in his own right. He wears a uniform fit for his title and I don't miss the multiple war medals that lay upon the left side of his chest. I inhale sharply as I gaze into the most amazing green eyes I have ever seen and he produces a wondrous smile as he leans forward into a low bow to address me, "Your Highness."*

A little giggle escapes my lips as I drop into another curtsy and return his greeting. It cannot be... I hear a huff from my left and I know my inappropriate reaction has displeased my father. I'm sure I'll hear about it later.

The young Prince steps forward and clears his throat. "Your Majesty," he says as he produces another bow. "Please allow me to introduce myself, I am Prince Theodore Ashton Johnson of Cambridge. As my father mentioned, if your daughter and I were to wed, we could put an end to the tension between our territories, be allies. My father will acknowledge the union for the remainder of his reign and sign a treaty to end the conflict.

This could be a prosperous opportunity for both our kingdoms. We could finally put an end to the squabble of old men past gone; and I am honoured to offer myself as a potential suitor for your daughter."

I turn and wait patiently for my father's reply, however he is just staring at the Prince with uncertainty in his eyes. My excitement begins to fray with his continued silence and I watch as he rubs his chin and leans back in his chair. He is going to say no! Suddenly, my father glances my way and subtly nods. I don't believe it, he is allowing me to decide for myself.

Not wanting to seem too eager and give anything away, I fold my hands in front of me and take a step forward. "Thank you, Your Highness, for your gracious offer. You have piqued my interest and I would like to hear more about what our kingdoms are capable of together. Would you care to take a walk with me in the gardens, so we may discuss this further?" Excitement is coursing through me, but I was born to be Queen and I will show my father I am capable of being one.

"I would like that very much," he responds happily, while his father smiles at the both of us.

"Well Howard, how about you and I go have a drink while these two love birds discuss the future?"

"You're insufferable Fillis," my father drawls as he stands and walks down the steps, away from his throne.

"I know." King Johnson chortles with glee as they both head for the side door.

"*Your Highness?*" *The Prince offers his arm and I walk down the few steps to link my arm through his. My heart is beating so fast I can barely contain my excitement.*

My guards follow us out to the edge of the gardens and once there, I turn and wave them away. They will keep watch from a distance while allowing me to have a little privacy.

When we are finally out of earshot, I slow our pace. "Am I dreaming?" I ask with butterflies swirling around in my stomach.

"No, my love. This is real."

"This doesn't seem real... You said you were a soldier in the King's army, I don't understand."

"Well, technically I am a soldier in the King's army." He gives me that smirk I love so much and continues. "I didn't disclose who I was because I wanted to be seen for who I am and not what I am. I never expected to fall for you the way I did... It appears though, that I wasn't the only one concealing their identity. You are definitely no maid."

"I never said I was, I just dressed like one. Although I did say I was stuck under the King's command. I'm to become Grandessa's new Queen, I have no choice in the matter... See why I could never leave."

"Yes, I can."

For a few minutes we walk through the gardens in complete silence, our attention on my mother's prize-winning roses.

"Did you mean what you said weeks ago, under the old oak tree, that if something were to change and we could actually be together, that we would be?" I ask, turning to face him as I place my hands on his biceps and he rests his hands on my hips. I don't care what the guards are probably thinking right about now, it's just me and him.

"I meant every word. You are my whole heart Cordelia and I never want to be away from you again." He gazes lovingly down at me while I smile back at him.

"I feel the same way."

"It's definitely going to take me some time to get used to calling you Cordelia," Theodore says with a smile on his face, rubbing the back of his neck.

"It's ok, it's going to take me a while too," I giggle. "So, we're really going to do this?"

"Absolutely, which reminds me." Theodore slides his hand into his jacket pocket and produces a black ring box. "This is a gift that I brought for you. I was originally going to come find you, before I made any formal proposal to the Princess. I needed you to know how much you meant to me, even if we couldn't be

together. I wanted you to have something that would remind you of the love I have for you." Theodore lifts my hands and places the small box within my palms. He then reaches forward and flips the lid, revealing a beautiful emerald encrusted ring. I inhale sharply as I flick my eyes between the treasure and his face.

"Oh my gosh, Theodore! This is too much, even for me. I can't take this."

"Yes, you can and you will. My grandmother Ida bestowed it to me years ago and said that when I found the keeper of my heart to give it to her, to hold on to them and never let go. You have my heart Cordelia and I would like nothing more than to be your husband, to stand by your side and help you rule over this great nation." Theodore takes the ring from the box within my grasp and gets down on one knee.

He gazes up at me with the most beautiful smile spread across his face, as he takes my left hand within his right. "Cordelia ah..." He pauses as he realises he does not know my full name.

"Cordelia Rosie Tailor." I whisper, giggling like a small child.

"Thank you," he says and then begins again. "Cordelia Rosie Tailor, will you make me the happiest man in all the territories, by becoming my wife?"

My face splits into the biggest smile as all my dreams are coming true. The man who owns my heart is kneeling before me, offering me a lifetime of happiness and I am more than willing to jump for it. A happy tear slips down my cheek as I whisper, "Yes."

As my mother finishes her tale, she wipes a happy tear from her face and the emerald green ring from her story catches the light from where it lies on her left hand. She smiles down at me and says, "So you see, if your father turned out to only be a commoner, we would not be where we are today. I do not want you to experience the same heartache I went through and that is why we must abolish the marriage law. That way you have a chance to find love on your own, just like I did."

That's all for now....

JOIN KRISTEN'S READER GROUP!

To stay up to date with any new releases